Even Villains Go To The Movies

LIANA BROOKS

OTHER WORKS

HEROES AND VILLAINS

Even Villains Fall In Love
Even Villains Go To The Movies
Even Villains Have Interns
Even Villains Play The Hero (books 1 – 3 omnibus)
The Polar Terror

TIME AND SHADOWS MYSTERIES

The Day Before
Convergence Point
Decoherence

FLEET OF MALIK

Bodies In Motion
Change of Momentum
For Every Action (forthcoming)

ALL I WANT FOR CHRISTMAS

All I Want For Christmas Is A Werewolf
All I Want For Christmas Is A Reaper

SHORTER WORKS

Darkness and Good
Fey Lights
Prime Sensations

Find other works by the author at www.lianabrooks.com.

EVEN VILLAINS GO TO THE MOVIES

LIANA BROOKS

AUSTRALIA

Print ISBN: 978-1-925825-94-7
eBook ISBN: 9781513058610

www.inkprintpress.com

National Library of Australia Cataloguing-in-Publication Data
Brooks, Liana 1982—
Even Villains Go To The Movies
176 p.
ISBN: 978-1-925825-94-7
Inkprint Press, Canberra, Australia
1. Fiction—Superheroes 2. Fiction—Romance—Science Fiction

Summary: Theoretically-retired supervillain Evan Smith must decide which he wants more: the world, or the woman he loves.

Second Edition: July 2015
Cover Artist: Victoria Miller
Editor: Jayne Wolf

For the unsung heroes.

CHAPTER ONE

Dear Mom,

New York is everything I hoped it would be. I love this school! Last semester alone the students showed a marked improvement over the previous year. And, so far, we haven't had a single senior drop out. This might be our highest graduation rate ever.

I'm really excited by all the improvements. It makes me feel like I'm actually doing something useful. I'm in control of myself, and it's wonderful.

The date with Simon was less exciting. He's... um... 'Dull as a brick' might be the right term. You'd think it would be easy to find someone who could carry on an intelligent conversation in New York, especially with Internet dating. It's 2032! But, no, this hypothesis has been proven incorrect yet again.

Give my love to Daddy, Gideon, and the minions. If Maria stops by, tell her I'm worried about her. Delilah and I talked about staging an intervention. I'm not sure, but Delilah thinks Maria will calm down once the shock of losing Martin is over. It may be just a phase.

APRIL IN NEW YORK City. Angela could almost taste the coming summer. She'd even rolled the car windows down to take advantage of the first warm day while she drove back from lunch. Summer would be bliss: eight weeks kid-free that she planned to fill by maxing out her tourist quota and hitting every landmark in a day's drive. By the time her second year as a teacher began in August, she would know more about New York than any native-born city slicker.

Angela parked her car and rolled the windows up. The school was experiencing an unprecedented surge in academic reform, but that didn't mean she needed to tempt the alumni with an easy steal.

A police siren screamed in the distance, echoing the fear and despair radiating from the school. It felt like the first edge of trouble, a nudging headache that made her want to snarl despite her good mood—but New York was like that, the underlying anger of the citizens scraping against her nerves until she was emotionally raw.

Public School 84 was hers though. Angela had been there long enough that she'd been able to slowly shift the mood of the school from fearful resentment to an amiable interest in learning. It was probably just a schoolyard punch-up, nothing to worry over too much.

Sipping on her smoothie, Angela headed for the impressive security array that divided the outside world from the inner sanctum of PS 84. Outside there were guns, drugs, and chaos. Beyond the arch of metal that scanned for everything from weapons to lethal viruses, there were regimented schedules, dusty deadwood copies of Shakespeare's sonnets, and young minds ready to argue over every word she said.

One of her favorite students had spent an hour debating the merits of shoelaces. You couldn't buy that kind of doublethink.

The security guard wasn't at her usual place in the main lobby, but Angela knew the drill. She swiped her ID, scanned her fingerprint, and headed for the lunchroom where there was undoubtedly a fight emerging.

As she neared the cafeteria, however, fear washed over her like the noxious smell of a skunk in the dark. Angela tossed her unfinished smoothie in the trash and thought of pleasant things. Bluebonnets on the Texas prairie, the smell of hot apple cider on a crisp winter night, the laughter of her baby brother, the love of her parents... She took it all, wrapping it into the idea of what her school should feel like.

At first, the collective mind of the students fought back. They were scared, and fear was a familiar friend. But she pushed, and they swayed under her will. Manipulating emotions was right up there with the ability to generate polka dots on a wall in terms of usefulness; unless she wanted to turn people into mindless slaves, there was very little she could do as far as the government was concerned. Besides, brute force wasn't her style.

Influencing things was different though. This is different, she told herself. She turned the corner into the cafeteria and almost jumped at the sight of Travys Freeman—top student in her AP calculus class—holding a gun.

The security guard had her Taser out and was trying to talk Travys into handing over the weapon. Terror so thick it was almost a physical force rolled off Travys. There was no way he would hand over anything to the guard. He wanted to turn it on himself. He just hadn't worked up the nerve. Yet. Waiting would be fatal for someone.

Angela cleared her throat and pushed on the mob. Everyone turned, even Travys. She smiled winningly. "This isn't about the quiz yesterday, is it?" she asked, weaving between the tables.

Travys made eye contact. Big mistake. Eye contact meant she had his full attention, and once she had that, he was hers.

"Travys, I asked you a question."

"It's not about the quiz, Miss Smith." The gun wavered, not quite dropping, but he wasn't sure where to aim.

Angela laid a comforting hand on the security guard's arm. "We don't need an audience do we, Travys?"

He shook his head.

"Miss Netley, why don't you get everyone to class? The bell is ringing," Angela added as the bell marking the end of lunch rang out. The crowd stayed frozen, spellbound by the same power that kept Travys from pulling the trigger. It was risky, but she refocused, encouraging everyone to hurry away. "Everyone go to class. Not you, Travys. I want a word with you."

The security guard shook herself out of her stupor. "Come on people, get to class. What are you gawking at?"

Conversation hummed to life around her and Travys sagged. The terror that had buoyed him was gone—only crushing despair remained.

Angela took a seat across the cafeteria table from him as the students and teachers filed out. Some of them tried to stay, or shout, or intervene, but she kept them all walking.

Travys peeked up at her, brown eyes filled with tears. "I'm sorry, Miss Smith."

"Guns don't solve anything. You know that."

He was getting ready to kill himself. She could feel it. The desire to stop the pain overwhelmed him. Angela tried to bleed it off, taking some of the despair herself. It hurt.

"What happened? You can tell me, Travys." She pushed thoughts of safety towards him. He wanted to believe, but Travys had no memories of safety. When they'd first met, he was a failing student, a scrawny sixteen-year-old who flinched when anyone raised their voice. Her power allowed her to create a sanctuary in the classroom, and in that sheltered place, he'd bloomed into a brilliant student.

"Did you get a college rejection letter?" she asked. It seemed the most probable answer.

He jerked his head to the side as if he'd been slapped. "Chris came home."

She sucked in air so fast it whistled past her teeth. "I thought he was doing twenty to life?"

"He got off on a technicality." Chris Freeman was his son's worst nightmare. He was a dealer with an anger problem who saw his only kid as a punching bag. Angela had never met the man, although she'd wanted to rearrange his brain after meeting Travys's mother, a sweet woman who was the poster child for domestic abuse.

"What's your mom doing?"

Travys's eyes dropped to the floor. "She didn't come home from work."

Which made her smarter than Angela thought. "Maybe she didn't know he was coming home."

"She knew."

And crueler than she'd guessed: she'd abandoned her son to a monster. "I'm sorry."

"I'm not going home," Travys said. His thoughts turned back to the gun. Angela could feel his longing for an escape.

"Shooting yourself won't make anything better."

He startled.

"Give me the gun. We'll make other plans for tonight. You won't go back home to him."

Travys hesitated.

"Give me the gun, Travys." She seized at his mind, making him want to please her. The desire for her approval was false—Travys was too strong-minded to need outside approval—but it worked. His arm lifted slowly, like he was fighting gravity.

"You can trust me."

"Nobody move, NYPD!"

Angela jumped. She'd been too focused on Travys to feel the approach of the police. In a split-second decision, she released her hold on Travys and reached out for the minds of the police before they could ruin everything.

It was the wrong decision.

Travys screamed in pain. His hand convulsed around the gun, pulling the trigger, and sending a bullet through the flesh of her upper arm.

Still trying to grasp the collective mind of the

police, everything blurred and Angela found herself standing near the main office in the arms of a strange man in bright green spandex.

"Travys! Hold still!" The police were moving, too focused for her to grasp; they'd stunned and cuffed Travys before she could even figure out what had happened.

She tried to brush the man aside. "Let me go." Angela released Travys's mind and focused on herself. The man in bright green held her.

"We need to get you to the doctor," the man said.

Angela realized he wasn't holding her as much as trying to hold her arm. Blood seeped between his gloved fingers. She blinked at it. The pain was secondary to the emotional savaging she'd taken from Travys's mind.

"Stay calm. An ambulance is on the way," the man repeated. He was trying to make eye contact. She didn't cooperate with him.

"I'll be fine. I'd like to check on my students now."

"If I hadn't rushed to your rescue, you would be dead." Confusion tinged his voice, as if he was waiting for praise.

She glared at the team hustling Travys out of the school. "If the police hadn't burst in here screaming, Travys would have handed the gun over and I wouldn't have been shot." She pushed him away. "This is your fault."

"No," said a crisp, authoritative female voice. "This is your fault."

Angela turned to look at the newcomer, an older woman with salt-and-pepper hair and a grim expression, which she recognized from a picture. Katrina Bocks, de facto government employee and chief of the United Nations Council for Superhero Control.

Not a friend.

"Miss Smith, please let the EMT examine your arm, and then I have some paperwork for you to sign."

"What sort of paperwork?" She wouldn't qualify to sign with the teachers' union until she'd worked a full school year, and she doubted the school board was prepared for this kind of situation. Besides, the chances that The Company was involved with something as benign as arranging medical leave were astronomically low. She'd sooner believe in love at first sight.

Katrina gave her a bitter smile, her emotions colored by hate and anger so violent it was almost a physical aura around her. "How long have been aware of your superpowers, Miss Smith?"

Angela played innocent. "Superpowers? I'm a teacher, but that's a generous compliment. Though some days I can't imagine anything harder than twisting these young minds around calculus." She widened her eyes, the very picture of an innocent southern belle.

Katrina wasn't buying it. She held up an old-style thumb drive. "I have papers saying you are a superhero with the ability to perform psychic manipulation."

"I don't believe anyone can do that."

"I also have evidence that you and the young man were in a very unprofessional relationship. When he came to his senses and realized how he'd been used, he came to school to kill you. The public will be incensed to hear you lived." Satisfaction edged Katrina's words. She thought she had Angela pinned in a corner.

The woman had come far too well-prepared. Angela looked over at the EMT hovering behind them. Time for a quick getaway. "I think I need to see the doctor now."

"I'll wait with you," the man offered. "For your protection."

Right, he was her well-meaning bodyguard, another concerned citizen fighting for truth, justice, and the American way. Angela moved to walk past Katrina, then stopped. "How long have you been tracking me?"

"I learned several months ago that a mind-raper was in the area. I didn't know who it was until today."

Angela nodded. Considering they didn't know the name of their target, they had certainly put a plan together quickly. Daddy was not going to like hearing about this. There was always a risk of The Company stumbling across her path this close to headquarters, but things had been so quiet lately she'd been sure she was flying under the radar. "I'll meet you at the hospital, I suppose?"

Katrina smiled triumphantly. "Yes. There's some very simple paperwork you need to fill out. And then we'll discuss more of your future after your surgery."

Her arm stung at the reminder. "I don't think I need surgery, just stitches."

"And I don't think a mutant should be allowed to breed," Katrina said. "Fortunately, the government sees my point of view. A quick snip-snip and you'll be safe to release into the wild."

Angela turned to follow the EMT, teeth clenched hard enough to hurt. There were so many things she wanted to say. None of them would help. Training took over, memories of summer drills under the hot Texas sun. The Company could come at any time. There was no hope of fighting them, so you had to evade, dodge, run.

She let the EMT load her into the back of the ambulance and waited until they'd hit the first stoplight before she dialed the only number that mattered. "Mom, they found me. Come pick me up."

CHAPTER TWO

Dear Mom,

The doctor says I can get the stitches out in a few weeks. There's going to be a scar, but that's what happens when a bullet takes a bite out of your arm. I might need physical therapy after the stitches come out, but it will have to wait until I can get a job here. Maria was able to sell my bike for a reasonable price so I have rent money for a bit and a new name. AJ David; it sounds like something out of a buddy-cop movie. Any minute now some burly old guy will break in and tell me he's two days from retirement.

Anyways, yes, I'll be able to find a job here. Just not teaching, for obvious reasons. Is it wrong to pray that your former boss will accidentally drop into a pit of lava?

It's L.A.—you'd think there'd be jobs everywhere but I can't find anything. Teaching is out until The Company backs off, and apparently blonde waitresses are a dime a dozen. I'm seriously tempted to cheat and force someone to hire me. I tell myself that I couldn't live with that in the long run, but every night I eat ramen noodles I seriously consider world domination. It's so easy. People want to do what I say, if I want them to. And... Well. I'll think of something.

Tell Daddy I say thank you for the allowance. I know he said it was my birthday money a little bit early, but since he'll send a birthday gift too, it's a loan. I'll pay you guys back when I get a job.

Love,
Angela

LOS ANGELES WAS ON the short list of places Angela had hoped never to live. Now, staring at the criminally beige walls of the cheapest apartment she could find, she listened to the L.A. traffic and an argument in Spanish from next door. A door slammed, and with a resigned sigh, Angela grabbed a plate of cookies. She stepped into the communal hall to see which one had retreated.

Luiz, single mom and neighbor, grimaced. "Sorry."

"Cookie?" Angela offered.

Luiz grabbed one and took Angela's unspoken invitation to step inside. They sat at the white plastic table Angela had found on the roadside as Luiz chewed her cookie angrily. "It wasn't supposed to be like this. We came out here to get away from my ex, be near family. My brother and I started a stunt company. We've got a good reputation, but the past few months." She shook her head as she stared at some personal nightmare. "Mikey said he had a big job, something that would set us up. He quit showing up to work, and now he's been arrested on a DUI. I'm so stressed and I'm always yelling at Mia. She's right. I'm a horrible mom."

"No, you aren't." Angela reached over and rubbed her shoulder. "She didn't mean that. Mia's a good kid, she loves you."

"She's failing classes."

Fights between Luiz and her daughter Mia revolved around two things: Mia's grades, and Mia's string of good-for-nothing boyfriends. Angela had heard every single fight for the past week. "Is she not doing the homework, or does she not understand the subject?"

"She says she doesn't understand." Luiz wiped tears from her face. "I just want something better for her. I don't want her to wind up like me."

Angela took a cookie. "Do you want me to tutor her?"

Luiz studied her suspiciously.

Being the only blue-eyed blonde in an area heavily populated by Latinos, Angela had gotten used to the looks of suspicion and contempt. She'd gotten the same response when she'd gone to high school in Laredo while her dad taught at the university for two years. She'd also picked up enough border-style

Spanish to make the fights all too easy to understand.

"I can't pay you," Luiz finally said.

"Let me borrow your bike so I can interview for jobs a couple times a week. That would be payment enough."

Luiz mulled it over, grabbing another hot cookie. "You can ride?"

"I have an M1 license, but I sold my bike when I left New York." It was sell the bike for cash or tell the school, and thereby The Company, where to send her last paycheck. She'd opted for selling the bike and twisting Delilah's arm until her sister used her security firm mojo to produce a new life for her under the name Angela Jane David.

Luiz's eyes narrowed. "How long have you been riding?"

"Since I was eighteen. Mom wouldn't let me have a bike when I was living at home." She shrugged.

Luiz drummed her fingers on the table. "If I can get you a job, you'd tutor my daughter so she doesn't fail classes?"

"I can tutor her so she understands what she's doing in class. Failing and passing are up to her. I can't magically make her a perfect student." Angela saw a mother's fear in Luiz's eyes. It rose off the heat of her skin like a perfume. "I'm a good tutor. I've done it before to pay bills."

"I know something you can do. The pay isn't tops, but it'll cover your groceries for the week." She stood. "I'll pick you up at seven. Wear riding gear, black if you have it. Try to act tough."

* * *

Arktos landed on the roof of the US Bank Tower in a corona of cold blue fire as the sun sank into the Pacific Ocean. He was late, again. He wanted to run his hand through his hair in frustration, but the mask he wore, the one that lent him better night vision and kept his features hidden while he worked, covered his head. The thieves had pulled off another jewel heist last night, and he wasn't any closer to tracking them down.

He walked to the edge of the building, looking down at the City of Angels from over a thousand feet up. People scurried around, wrapped in their own worries, insulated by their private fears and precious egos. Somewhere in that mess were the three people he wanted.

They were getting better.

The first heist had been badly executed, and it was only because the police hadn't called The Company for help that he hadn't caught them then. It was frustrating that a set of amateurs who couldn't plan ahead enough to take care of a silent alarm were still smart enough to wear masks and gloves.

Their second heist had been better planned. The woman had acted as a distraction. A car wreck, an armored car blocked in traffic, and then the fire bug in the group had bombed the truck, grabbed the cash, and they were gone. His only hint had been a flash of blonde under the woman's USC Trojans baseball cap.

A blonde woman with the ability to influence emotions fit the description of the mind-raper who'd escaped The Company in New York. It wouldn't be the first time a rogue had teamed with a villain, and it wouldn't be the last. And if they had kept to hitting stores and trucks, he wouldn't be so worried. Last night's heist though—that had been different. The mind-raper had held an entire restaurant in thrall while the heist team robbed them blind.

That twist left him with a sick feeling in his stomach and the urge to freeze the criminals in their tracks. His fingers tingled as frost settled around him. Even in the spring heat, he was cold.

Arktos leapt from the building, letting the rush of air strip away his worries. On the edge of thought, he could feel the tug of an idea. A vision appeared, a hazy overlay of the city, and he saw the studio.

With a chuckle, he barrel-rolled in the sky, switching directions high above the streets and heading for home. Sometimes his premonitions let him see something that was about to happen, like the first heist that he'd called in to the police. And sometimes it acted like an alarm clock to make sure he got to work on time. A subtle reminder from his subconscious that he needed to get to work if he wanted to get paid.

CHAPTER THREE

Dear Mom,

L.A. is even weirder than I thought it would be. I miss Texas, but I have a job...

Love,
Angela

HOLLYWOOD MAGIC CREATED A strip of alley wide enough for a motorcycle gang to roar down in the middle of a giant room that seemed to be mostly places for lights and cameras to hang.

Angela took off her helmet and wiped sweat from her eyes. Fog roiled around her feet, giving the impression of a winter chill, but the glaring lights were hot. At the far end of the alley, two men argued over something, a camera angle maybe. She glanced at Luiz for direction.

Originally she'd thought she was coming along to play Luiz's assistant, make a coffee run or three, but Luiz had introduced her as the stuntwoman AJ David. She'd flashed a couple of cards and told Angela to sign all the paperwork as fast as she could. Angela made a mental note to make sure she had all the proper licenses, permits, guild cards, and union paperwork done by morning. There were rules in Hollywood, and she was certain she'd broken about fifty unwritten ones. Hopefully Daddy could fake a California accent long enough to play her agent if anyone called.

"They're going to make us do it again," one of the men said. Angela thought his name was Dyfed, but she wasn't sure. Luiz was riding as the gang leader, doing tricks that made Angela's heart stop. Dyfed and Michael were a set of twins who did jumps. Angela was paired with a woman named Raina who had told her their only job was to gun their motors and look fierce. Or as fierce as was possible with a helmet on.

Luiz glanced at her. "Welcome to show biz. It's a lot of hurry up and wait. They're trying to get the angles and lighting right before the talent shows up."

"Talent?"

"Movie stars," Raina said. "Try not to swoon like a girl."

Angela frowned but couldn't think of a decent reply.

"Glee!" the man on the other end of the set yelled.

"Patrick Swendon," Luiz said. "He's the director. If he tells you to do something, you nod and say, 'Yes, sir.'"

"Got it."

"Glee!" Swendon yelled again. "What are you doing there?" He was pointing at the 'gang'.

Angela turned around to see if anyone had joined them. It was just the five of them in black leather and a morass of confusion.

"You with the blonde hair!" Swendon shouted. "Earth to Glee! Get over here?"

"Um..." Luiz said.

Angela pointed to herself.

"Yes, you!"

She coasted her bike across the set, stopping just in front of a lean man who was on the wrong side of fifty and red from anger. "Yes, sir?"

"You're supposed to be riding with Tyler, remember? We went over that yesterday. Why are you down there with the gang?"

Angela bit her lip.

Luiz coasted up beside her. "Mr. Swendon, this is AJ David. She's one of my stunt riders."

The director glared at Angela. "Get off the bike and come over here." He turned and yelled at someone in the shadows behind him. "Get me my glasses! Where are my glasses? Thank you." After putting them on, he turned back to blink at Angela.

"You're not Glee's body double?"

She glanced at Luiz, who shook her head. "No, she's just a rider."

"We need to get her hair covered. It's almost a perfect match for Glee's wig." His eyes narrowed. "How tall are you?"

"Five ten," Angela said.

He sighed in disappointment. "Too bad. You would make a perfect body double if you weren't so tall. Glee's at least four inches shorter than you."

"They're probably the same height if Glee's in her heels and AJ's wearing flats," Luiz put in helpfully. *Job*, she mouthed to Angela.

The director nodded. "How are you with mouthy, temperamental women who like to rage at the world?"

"I have sisters," Angela said. No regular human being could ever match Maria throwing a tantrum. Normal humans couldn't throw lightning and turn enemies to piles of ash when they were in a bad mood.

"Good enough. Where's Tyler's body double? What's his name?" The director stormed off into the shadows.

A motorcycle pulled up beside her, fire engine redand ridden by a tuxedoed man. Jet black eyes matched jet black hair. He had a strong jaw and dark skin, but not the right bone structure for a Latino. He was disconcertingly familiar.

She tipped her head to the side trying to decide where she'd seen him before. At the store maybe? Or on TV?

"Tyler!" Swendon huffed. "We aren't ready for you."

"I'm done with makeup, there aren't any lines, and all you need is a shot of me rolling down the alley with a blonde hanging on. Why don't we shoot this and call the scene done?"

Angela tried to remember if she'd ever heard of an actor named Tyler. It didn't ring any bells.

"Glee said she wanted to do this," Swendon argued.

"Glee's still in her trailer trying to memorize her lines for the next scene." Tyler gave Angela a look usually reserved for cockroaches right before they became a smear of entrails on the kitchen floor.

Angela shrugged it off. The big, muscled types were all the same: lots of bulk and no brains. He'd probably played football in high school, and she knew enough football players to gag at the thought of ever spending another night watching men run around in tights.

"Fine," Swendon said. "We'll get the lights in place. Roll down the main drag with the body double. Somebody go find Glee! Tell her she has five minutes!"

Tyler scowled down at her. "Well? Are you going to ask for an autograph?"

Several snippy rejoinders came to mind, but instead Angela smiled. "Naturally, as soon as I see an actor I like."

He blinked.

Angela stopped herself from rolling her eyes. "Where am I supposed to be?"

He got on his bike and looked at her over his shoulder. "Hop on."

She climbed on behind him, carefully avoiding the name of the position she was in. There might not have been the Fear of God in her house growing up, despite being in the Bible Belt, but there was certainly the Fear of Grandmother Meredith. As in, "What would your grandmother say?!?" or "Your Grandmother Meredith must be rolling in her grave!" Although Mom had stopped using that when Dad had snapped back, "All seven of them."

Dad had never thought highly of Grandma Meredith, and she'd died before Angela had ever met her, but the specter of the proper southern woman lived on. Southern Ladies did not say Certain Words.

Angela settled in, flipped her hair, and held the bike seat on either side of her thighs. It was that, or wrap her arms around tall, dark, and stupid.

"You're supposed to hold on," Tyler said.

"It's a test shot." She didn't move to grab him.

He revved the motorcycle, driving faster than necessary, weaving between barely visible marks on the floor that Luiz assured her would vanish in post-production. On his mark, Tyler pivoted the bike with precision control, and she had to grab his waist to keep from falling off.

"Told you so." He smirked.

Angela growled and flipped her hair again, aiming for his eyes. Tyler dodged. She slid off the bike and walked over to the camera crew. "Was that good enough? I'd rather drive myself."

The woman behind the camera nodded. "It's good. All we need is Glee and we can do the actual take." The woman gave her a conspiratorial grin. "What did you think of Tyler Running Fox? Does he smell good?"

"Tyler... Running Fox?" Angela looked over her shoulder at the biker who'd tried to hurl her to her death. "He's the one who ruined *Hamlet*? I didn't recognize him without the goatee."

The camerawoman choked on a laugh. "You didn't like his Hamlet? He won an Academy Award for that!"

"The screenwriters butchered Shakespeare's play. They didn't even get the 'To be or not to be' soliloquy right. It was painfully bad," she said as she became aware of someone looming over her shoulder.

Tyler Running Fox—Hollywood hero, Academy darling, the highest-grossing and most popular Native American actor ever—glared down at her.

"I don't like the way you drive, either," she said before she flounced back to her bike, well aware she wasn't going to act in Hollywood ever again.

CHAPTER FOUR

Dear Mom,

Tell Gideon I'm proud of him for getting into MIT. My alma mater won't know what hit it! I've already sent an email to my advisor warning her that my baby brother is on his way. She said she'd consider taking early retirement if he wants a math degree. On the other hand, she said that if he goes for an engineering degree like Dad she'll stick around just to watch the havoc. Apparently, Dr. Trenbel in engineering gave her a hard time while I was there and she would like, and I quote, "To let him try and handle a Smith!" I'm sure she means it with love.

I had a job for about eight hours, but I don't think I'll have a second shift. I'm trying to get worked up about it, but it wasn't anything more than riding a motorcycle. I miss teaching.

Have you heard anything about Travys? I tried to find out what happened while I was at the library, but I can't find a mention of him in the system. Could The Company bury a trial like that?

Love,
Angela

"OKAY, THAT'S WHERE YOU'RE wrong," Angela said as she leaned over Mia's shoulder to scrutinize her homework. "A squared plus B squared is C squared, and you forgot to take the square root of the total." She reached over and put a little square root sign over the number sixteen. "See?"

"I can't do math!" Mia flopped forward like a marionette with her strings cut. "When will I ever use this? Tell me when I will ever need to calculate the lengths of the side of a triangle."

"When you're a famous architect designing the next great skyscraper?" Angela suggested. "Or when you're an artist working on proportions. Everything involves math. Here"—she scribbled the Pythagorean Theorem on Mia's paper—"this is fun. It's super easy, plug-and-play math."

"Math is not fun," Mia grumbled.

"It can be."

"It really can't."

"What if I add one chocolate chip to the cookie dough for every answer you get right?"

Mia eyed her homework. "Make it three, or we're still going to have chipless chocolate chip cookies."

Angela nodded. "Three per correct answer. I'll take one away for every one I have to help on." She stretched her legs out and basked in the California sunshine. The AC was wheezing inside, but outside a nice ocean breeze cooled the city streets. A nice something breeze, at any rate. The fog had lifted, the city buzzed around them, and Angela felt safe dipping into the public mood for a minute to check how her neighborhood was doing.

It was a little like gardening. She didn't need to pay attention to everything that was going on all the time. Like checking the flowers and pulling the occasional weed, she checked on the general mood of the area every few days to ensure everything was running smoothly.

Today the area was happy. Spring sunshine and a clear sky were enough to perk up anyone's mood. There were a few hints of anger, and one of deep despair, but they were close enough that she could touch them at a distance and alter them, turning anger to patience and despair to humor. Later, she decided, she'd go for a run and check on Despair. It felt like a severe case of postpartum, but she couldn't remember seeing any new mothers in the area.

Not that this was a friendly neighborhood. Nothing like the little town in Texas she'd spent most of her time in. On the lakes of LBJ there was a quiet retirement community, a few young families, and typical Southern nosiness. Between her father's charm, the novelty of being a quad, and her own forceful personality, she'd known everything about everyone.

LA had tabloids and gossip, but it all centered around the same handful of people, as if the only measure of worth was money.

She leaned her head back, soaking up sunshine and the blissfully carefree life of the unemployed who had money for rent and groceries. Tomorrow, she'd be worried again. For today, she would patiently coax Mia into appreciating math and maybe hit the cupcake place to celebrate payday.

Splurging on cupcakes meant a ten-mile run, but what was the point of running if not to eat cupcakes every now and then?

Luiz bounced down the apartment steps. "AJ, what are you doing? We need to leave."

"What?"

"We have a night shoot, remember? We need to be there by five to start blocking out the fight scenes." Luiz was already wearing her riding gear—tight black faux leather pants, a tight yellow shirt, and a faux leather jacket cropped short, her helmet dangling from her hand. "You signed the contract."

"I insulted the 'talent' last night too," Angela said, miming the air quotes. "I don't think they want me back."

"Did someone call you and tell you not to show up?"

Angela raised her eyebrows. "No phone, remember? I'm broke."

"Then get your gear on and get unbroke by getting your lazy self to work. You're worse than my brother."

"Oooo." Mia pretended to bite her nails in mock fear and then smiled. "You better go. She's serious."

Angela ran upstairs, stuffed her leathers in a backpack, and grabbed her helmet. She pulled the jacket on over her T-shirt that read 'Fight Like A Girl—Zephyr Girl.'

Luiz was waiting on her bike.

"I really need to buy my own transport," Angela muttered. "I hate holding on to people."

"Yeah, but holding on to Tyler can't be that much of a chore. I've seen his body. If he didn't look so much like my ex I'd make a play for that." Luiz revved the engine and sped into traffic before Angela could respond that the last thing she wanted to do was make a play for Tyler Running Fox.

They left black skid marks in the parking lot, but made it inside on time.

"We're doing the setup, not shooting," Raina said when Angela asked for a place to change. "You don't need to be in costume for that."

Their set was outside, a miniature city skyline with a scaled-down helo pad. Luiz started them out on some wrestling pads, working on stunt throws. "Have you ever danced, done karate, anything like that?"

"I had a blue belt in karate, but all I remember are the basic self-defense moves." Having her mom kidnapped when Angela was four by people who had wanted to murder them all had put her family on the defensive. Her sisters had done better with martial arts, Delilah going so far as to pick up a couple of extra disciplines, but Angela hadn't ever needed it. People didn't attack her. Anyone coming towards her got hit with a heavy dose of regret that sent them straight to their knees.

Luiz frowned. "Have Raina do a practice throw with you." She tugged at her black braid. "I wish my brother was here. He's always been the one upfront for stunt fights. Dyfed! Come 'ere."

"It's easy," Raina said. "Stand like this and pretend you're holding my arm while I flip."

Angela rested a hand on her and Raina somersaulted in the air, landing flat on her back. "Are you okay?"

"AJ, it's a stunt, I'm supposed to land like this."

"Right."

Raina stood. "Let's try throwing you. When I touch your back, I want you to fall forward like I pushed you hard. Ready? One, two, three..."

Angela felt the light tap of Raina's fingers on her back and flung herself at the mat. "Oww."

"A little less enthusiastic next time."

Luiz whistled. "Everybody take ten minutes and get water, stretch out. I'm going to block out the fight scene with the director."

"I thought it was blocked," Raina said. "Didn't we go over this last week?"

"There's been a change."

Angela wandered over to the sideboard full of food. As she shrugged on her leather jacket someone said, "Nice shirt. I like Zephyr Girl."

She turned. A handsome, dark-skinned man faced her, giving her elevator eyes. Her shirt must have riveted him, because his gaze never got above her neck.

"I'm a fan of hers," Angela said as she pulled her jacket all the way on and zipped the front. It was too hot for a leather jacket, but she didn't like his stare. A little stand-offish body language was in order.

Luiz swore loudly in Spanish and stalked over. "I swear on my mother's grave, I am ten seconds from quitting this contract and calling it a day. This is not the only studio in Hollywood, it's just the most—" She stopped and scowled at the newcomer. "What are you doing here?"

He picked up a donut. "I heard you had the good food."

"I thought principal shooting was done for you guys."

He shrugged. "We had an emergency meeting to discuss issues." He gave Luiz a wicked grin. "Want to hear some good gossip?"

Luiz grabbed a flimsy plate and piled it high with potato chips. "Lay it on me."

"The TV show *Fractured*? It's getting canceled."

"What?"

He held his hands up in a shrug of surrender. "You heard it here first. Carla didn't show up for her promo scenes yesterday. This afternoon she called to say she's buying herself out of her contract. No Carla, no Pacifica, no *Fractured*."

Angela watched the exchange with morbid fascination. It was like discovering a new continent. All the words were ones she should understand, but the dialect was foreign.

Luiz must have seen her befuddled expression because she laughed. "AJ, this is Jacob Kapsimolis. He's a superhero."

She took an involuntary step backward. "Really?" A Company employee in Hollywood was not what she needed.

"I'm the Red Death on *Fractured*," Jacob said. He flung his arms forward. "I'll have my revenge!"

Angela's heart skipped a beat, and then she realized he was acting. "Oh. That was... was good. I've seen the show a few times. I like it," she added lamely. She'd seen half an episode in the airport and it hadn't been horrible.

Jacob looked pleased, then shrugged. "Except, as of tomorrow, I'll officially be another unemployed actor begging for coffee money. Who are you?"

"She's the new stunt double," Luiz said.

"I heard about you." A grin lit up his face. "The one who hates *Hamlet*, right? Sweet! I can't stand Shakespeare."

"AJ David, stuntperson." She held out her hand. "And I do like Shakespeare, but not the way Ty—"

Jacob bulldozed over her introduction. "Speaking of stuntpeople, where's your brother, Luiz? I was hoping he could help me drown my woes."

"He got a DUI while on probation," Luiz snapped. "I ain't paying the bail, so he's rotting in the clink." She took a drink from her water bottle. "Do you ever feel like this studio is a breath away from collapsing in on its own stupidity? Studio Sluts will be the death of us all."

"Studio Sluts?" Angela asked.

"Glee was a Studio Slut," Luiz said. "She got her first part because she was sleeping with the owner, his latest bit of tit. The movie should have tanked, but she was perfect for the part and stole the show. The studio signed her on a six-year earn-out contract—she had to star in a movie which grossed a certain amount, or continue acting in the movies until she hit that point. This is her third and the contract's up in six months; the only way it will gross anything is because Tyler is here."

"Carla is Glee's replacement," Jacob said. "When Glee's second movie tanked, her sugar daddy dropped her and picked up another young thing. He's the one who bought out her contract with *Fractured*, I guarantee it. Carla has never had that kind of money."

"And now Glee has decided she won't be shooting any of the stunts because she's afraid of heights."

Luiz rolled her eyes. "Two weeks ago she threw an almighty tantrum because Swendon brought in a body double. Now she's flip-flopping, tonight's shoot might get canceled."

Angela picked up a water bottle. "Maybe—OW!" She flailed as someone pulled her backward by her hair.

"Give me the wig!"

Angela rounded on the woman tugging at her hair. "What on earth are you doing?"

CHAPTER FIVE

Dear Mom,

Don't worry about sending money. I've found a job and my first paycheck comes before the end of the month. If Delilah calls to ask you about a Rembrandt, tell her you're not interested. There's a new exhibit coming to the museum and she was going to go birthday shopping for you.

Remember the da Vinci she picked up for you when we went on that trip to Paris our sophomore year? It's going to be like that all over again.

Your law-abiding daughter,
Angela

ANGELA RUBBED HER SCALP, scowling at the woman who'd yanked on her hair.

"I need Glee's wig if we're going to film this scene," the pinched-faced woman said with a puckered glower.

Luiz batted the woman away. "That's her real hair, Kerry. AJ, this is the wardrobe director for this disaster. Kerry, AJ, she's filling in for my brother."

"No, I don't have a blonde you can borrow from me." Patrick Swendon stepped around the corner mid-argument with a slightly shorter, bald man. "Kerry, where's the wig?"

"I don't need a wig," the other man argued. "I'll take your coffee girl. I just need someone who can pose in a white catsuit."

"Sweetie, you have a casting director, go ruin his day. I have enough problems."

The bald man put his hands on his hips. "You are so sleeping on the couch tonight!"

They both came to a stop in front of the buffet table. Swendon looked Angela up and down. "Can you jump off buildings?"

"Yes, sir."

"Good, you're Glee's new body double for stunts. Kerry will get your costume."

"Jacket off," Kerry ordered.

Angela obligingly unzipped the jacket and noticed the bald man's eyes fixed on her shirt. She resisted the urge to take a deep breath.

"Have you ever considered being a superhero?" Baldy asked.

Angela smiled shyly as she shook her head. "Not really."

"She's a fan of Zephyr Girl," Jacob said with a wink.

Swendon stepped in front of her. "No. Mine."

The bald man gave him a limpid-eyed look. "Oh, come now darling, you know you like threesomes."

Panicking, Angela turned to Luiz for help.

Luiz leaned over. "That's Patrick's husband, Geoff. He's also the producer and director for *Fractured*. Rumor has it that he's obsessed with the superheroes, especially Zephyr Girl."

Jacob was nodding eagerly, Geoff Swendon was already fawning, and Patrick seemed resigned.

Angela smiled shyly. "What do you need me to do?"

"All I need is a few days of filming, so we can edit Carla out and put you in as the superhero Pacifica. It's a blue and white catsuit, you'll look amazing," Geoff said with his hands folded in prayer.

"I need you to do Glee's stunts," Patrick said. "But it's mostly night shoots at this point."

Luiz held a hand up. "AJ is already under contract with my company. Patrick, if you want her you're going to need to call her agent and set up a separate contract for her. Right now she's here as a stunt rider and background character. Geoff, she can do some test shots with you tonight, but then you need to write up a contract."

Both men nodded eagerly and Angela sighed. Daddy was going to have way too much fun with this. And she was willing to bet that sleep wouldn't be in either of the contracts.

* * *

Arktos woke with a scream. A cold sweat covered his body as he fought off the nightmare that had woken him. A beautiful, red-haired woman approached a door, the door exploded, and her body was found in the cold dawn light. Again, and again, and again, the scene had repeated itself in his dreams until finally he'd fought to escape sleep.

After taking a deep breath, he climbed out of his over-sized bed and pulled on a pair of jeans. He went downstairs where a light was on in the kitchen.

His little brother Aaron looked up in confusion. "I thought you said you didn't have anything to do tonight."

"I couldn't sleep. Bad dreams."

"About Mom?"

Arktos shot his little brother a look that would have chilled the blood of most men. "No. It wasn't about anything real." He rooted around in the kitchen until he found a pitcher of lemonade. "What are you doing up?"

"Studying." Aaron sulked.

"You need to sleep too."

"It's only ten. I'm going to finish the practice worksheet for math and go to bed." Aaron worked in silence for a few minutes, portraying the Good Student with a skill that never went as far as the classroom. "I'm not going to get kicked out this time," he said when he caught Arktos watching. "My grades are good. I've even got a tutor."

"A tutor?" Arktos raised an eyebrow. "The last 'tutor' you had couldn't add two plus two."

"This one's different." He hesitated a moment. "My friend Mia has a tutor. She said I could come over and study with her this weekend."

"We'll see," Arktos said. He'd take Aaron over on his bike and see if there was an adult in the area before passing judgment. Taking a sip of his lemonade, he stared out the window to the dark garden and wondered if he should go for a run. Sleep wasn't going to come back easily and sitting in the kitchen held no appeal.

He turned to tell Aaron he was headed out when the vision caught him. It was an alley outside a conference hall that he knew. And there, the red-haired woman pulling up on a motorcycle. She parked the bike and sauntered down the alley, fully confident of her safety. She touched the door handle, and he felt the heat of the blast.

"Are you okay? Hey!" Aaron jumped out of his chair. "Are you okay?"

"I've got to go. There's going to be a problem downtown. Get to bed. I'll be back before you leave for school." He kissed Aaron's head before running out the door. "Get some sleep."

CHAPTER SIX

Dear Daddy,

The next time you suggest to the director that I replace the star of a show, I will drop scorpions in your Dior suit. Do not play innocent with me. There are rules in Hollywood, and one of those is that unknown girls who fill in as motorcycle stunt riders don't get offered jobs as lead actresses within twenty-four hours of getting their first job. Don't think I don't see your hand in all of this.

What I'd like to know is: Where did you hide the minions?

They're in the studio, aren't they? Lurking like the little monsters they are in the shadows? Are there minions at my house, Dad?

The minions can't eat intruders. This isn't Texas. California doesn't have the same home defense laws, and I really don't think your genetically altered minion is the same as a dog. That's going to be very hard to prove in court.

I love you, Daddy. I know you just want me to be happy. But can you please call the insane producer back and tell him

ANGELA TOSSED THE RED curls of her wig and parked Luiz's bike in the alley behind the conference center. She hadn't put on her Rage getup since arriving in L.A., but tonight the mental screams of terror echoing from the center warranted the kind of investigation that would attract questionable attention.

Tight black jeans, a bright red tank top that matched her hair, and a leather duster that was too heavy for the L.A. heat were a start. She'd added a black domino mask that obscured the shape of her nose and cheekbones when she'd moved to New York, because no one needed to see their favorite schoolteacher beating down the local thugs. The heart and star pendant around her neck—a little invention of Daddy's that would shield her from most things—completed the outfit.

The 'most' still worried her some days.

Terror radiated from the building, escalating until the headache tearing into her brain was a living fire. Whatever was happening, she would hit back. Hard.

Checking to make sure the alley was empty, Angela sauntered towards the back door and hoped someone inside had been kind enough to leave it open. More often than not the people hired to cater at these places would stick a rock in the door to keep it from locking every time they slipped out for fresh air.

If not, she could always pick the lock. Angela sighed. The whole point of moving away from her sisters was to avoid a life filled with crime and superheroes.

Angela reached for the door and someone hit her. A breeze ruffled her wig and she found herself on her back in the alleyway, staring up at a masked man. No hate tainted the aura around him; nothing that suggested that he was dangerous except that he was bigger than her.

She raised an eyebrow. "Hello?"

The man took a deep breath. "Hi." He smelled like mint.

"I'm new to the area, so I'm not familiar with the protocol when you're jumped by a masked man in an alleyway. Is there a secret handshake or something?" she asked sarcastically.

"I'm here to save your life."

Angela looked around for signs of danger. The man was the only thing in the alley, and he was cradling her, hand cushioning her head, muscular arm suspending him in a pushup so his body weight wasn't resting on her.

"Right. What danger am I in, exactly?"

"The door is going to explode and kill you," he said in a very serious tone.

She lifted her head to peer over his shoulder at the door. It was a mistake. The movement meant gyrating under him in his spandex suit, and she caught a whiff of cologne, soap, and clean sweat. His emotions shifted, becoming tinged with desire and arousal.

Angela cleared her throat and lay back down, trying to put space between herself and her captor. "Mmhmm. Tell you what, let me up and I'll help you find your doctor. I bet someone is very worried about you missing your medicine."

The man shook his head insistently. "I had a vision and saw you killed."

"And I had a vision where I won an all-expenses-paid trip to Fiji. That doesn't mean anything is going to happen. Let me get up, please."

"No. It's not safe."

Her patience frayed as the terror inside amped her headache up another notch. "I'm not lying here until I die of starvation because the door might—"

The door exploded.

Blue ice surrounded them like a shield, then, as the last piece of shrapnel fell to the ground in a smoldering pile, the ice receded, leaving frost patterns on the pavement.

"I told you so," the superhero said as he pushed himself up. He was taller than she was and his black costume had jagged blue lightning strikes crossed over it.

Angela smoothed her wig out. "Fine. You have visions. Are they anything useful, like winning lotto numbers?"

"It doesn't work like that."

"It never does." She eyed the smoking wreckage of the doorway. "Care to clean this up?"

"What am I, your maid?"

"And my nanny." Angela stepped towards the door.

"Who are you?"

She pointed. "Cool the hallway off, and I'll tell you."

The hero shot a jet of icy cold air down the wall. Melting metal cracked under the arctic blast.

"Very nice," Angela said, turning her back on him and studying the remains of the door. "Very nice indeed."

* * *

"Who are you?" Arktos repeated. Nothing in his vision had hinted at the fact that the woman would be another superhero. Or quite so... attractive. With their bodies pressed together he'd been far too aware of lithe muscles under him and the subtle spice of her citrus perfume. It clung to him like a phantom hand, stroking his libido.

She gave him a come-hither smile. "I'm Rage."

"Rage?"

"Because I manipulate emotions and enrage people?" She waited with an expectant smile. "It's sort of a joke."

"I've never heard of you."

"Under the circumstances I'm sure I can find it in my heart to forgive you."

He stretched an arm across the doorway, blocking her from stepping into the hall. "You need to go home now."

She patted his cheek. "You're so cute. How long have you been in the business? Three years? Four?"

"Six."

"I've been in it for over twenty, so let's pretend that I know what I'm doing and you're the newbie who still needs training pants. M'kay? Good. I'm glad we had this little talk." She fluttered her eyelashes at him before brushing past, trench coat swaying as she walked.

He stared. "No one has been with The Company for over twenty years. None of the talent, at least." Most heroes didn't survive four years. It was a rough life and he'd only made it so far because he was cautious. He had Aaron to think about.

She threw him a glance over her shoulder. "I didn't say I was with The Company. I said I was in the business."

"Rogue."

"I prefer the term freelance." She shot him a coy smile. "The pay is nothing to write home about, but I set my own hours."

"And what's your talent?"

"I can sense emotions."

He waited for her to add something. When she didn't respond, he jogged along the hall to catch up. "What else do you do?"

"Nothing," she said, resuming her brisk pace.

Arktos's eyebrows went up under his mask. "Do you even know what's going on in there?"

"I hear people screaming in pain and the door was booby-trapped. That's enough for me. It's giving me an ever lovin' headache."

He caught her shoulder and pulled her away from the balcony door. "I don't hear anything."

She didn't flinch under his gaze, or try to pull away. "I hear emotions like you hear words. Most people are just whispers; I can sense their emotion if I really try, but usually it's drowned out by the noise of my own thoughts. This is like having a rock concert under my bedroom window when I have a migraine. People in there are terrified. It's a sustained group emotion and getting worse. Something has them trapped, and some of them are about to die. The human body isn't capable of sustaining stress reactions for prolonged periods of time. It's damaging. Now, is this door going to explode?"

"I don't think so," Arktos said slowly.

"Good." Rage pushed the door open with exaggerated care and peeked inside. "Looks like a concert crowd. Maybe a benefit show of some kind?"

"Henry West was giving a speech here. It's not campaign season yet, but he likes to make the rounds to keep the donors interested."

Her smile was a little cruel. "Lots of old people with money?"

"That sounds about right."

"I see two people on stage. One of them's an emotional manipulator, but I can't tell which, they're too close."

Arktos leaned in, aware he was brushing against her body as he peeked inside. On stage was a blonde in a stunningly short red dress. Next to her stood a man wreathed in flames.

"I think the blonde's the mind-raper. I want to talk to her. She won't be able to manipulate me."

"Because you're special, right?"

He glared at her, trying not to smile when she didn't flinch. "Yes, because I'm special. See if you can get the pyro to hold still while I talk to the blonde."

"I have a better idea." She pulled her jacket off, revealing an angry red wound on her arm with fresh stitches. "Hold this." Tossing her red curls so they caught the light, Rage stepped into the room.

Arktos wasn't sure what he was expecting her to do, but as she moved he was hit by the overwhelming desire to stare at her. Rage fascinated him, the way the light caressed her fiery curls, the graceful curve of her hip. He imagined what her hand would feel like as it stroked him. How soft would her lips be when he kissed her?

He shook his head and refocused on the thieves. One of them was missing. There were always three: the blonde, the pyro, and the bagman who wore a mask. Where was their bagman?

"Attention, ladies and gentlemen! Hello!" Rage waved.

Everyone turned to face her, including the criminals. Arktos eased his way into the shadows by the door and headed for the mind-raper on the stage. Katrina from the head office had sent him a detailed description of the woman who'd molested a child and injured a police officer escaping from Bugman. He hadn't expected her to come here, but he wasn't surprised either. California attracted all sorts of freaks.

"Boys and girls, I hate to break up such a fun party, but Mommy and Daddy need some alone time now. Sweet cheeks"—Rage pointed at the blonde with her Prada bag, no doubt filled with stolen jewelry—"It's not Halloween, you shouldn't be trick-or-treating. Put it down."

The blonde dropped her bag of stolen goodies.

Arktos grabbed it. "Can you get the people out?" The pyro was shaking; if he lost control people would get hurt.

"Show's over!" Rage said.

A strong desire to head for his car washed over Arktos. Then fear, which was buffeted by lust, and followed by terror. The emotions grabbed at him, worse than any childhood night terror, pulling away his focus. Rage and the pyro stood toe-to-toe, staring at each other.

He edged toward the blonde, not quite able to take his eyes off Rage.

Fear made his mouth go dry.

Rage moved without warning, bringing her knee up and dropping the pyro with ball-aching accuracy.

His head cleared and he made a grab for the blonde, but she was already racing off through the crush of fleeing people.

The pyro groaned a curse. "I'm going to kill you."

Rage tilted her head to the side. "So sweet. We've just met and you're already offering me death threats. It's adorable."

"I'm not adorable!" The pyro lunged at Rage.

Arktos moved without thinking, diving between pyro and rogue and throwing up a shield of ice. It steamed.

Something dug into his shoulder. He rolled sideways to see Rage poking him with a booted foot.

"Are you always this overdramatic?"

"He was trying to kill you."

"So throw an ice cage over him, not me!"

"I was trying to protect you."

She rolled her eyes. "How adorably antiquated."

Arktos stood, brushing imaginary dust off his uniform. "I thought the pyro was adorable."

"The pyro is getting away."

He pivoted in time to see the pyro launch himself skyward. Arktos followed, chasing his quarry into the clouds and losing him high above the L.A. skyline. By the time he returned to the crime scene, Rage and her bike were gone.

CHAPTER SEVEN

Dear Mom,

I wish I could come home for the barbecue this weekend, but there's a thing I need to attend for the TV show I'm now acting in. I need a dress, if you have any that you think would fit.

Ever busy,
Angela

SCROLLING THROUGH THE SEARCH results on her phone was a less-than-ideal way to research. Angela bit into her apple and tried again to find anything about the superhero she'd bumped into, but the best she could find were references to a Roman legend about a centaur and the Greek word for 'bear.'

Arktos had darker skin, and maybe black hair— she thought she'd seen it curl out from under his mask. Dark skin, dark hair, a Greek name...

Jacob Kapsimolis winked at her as he swaggered off the set. "They're almost ready for you, gorgeous."

Angela rolled her eyes and finished her apple.

"Are you reading something dirty?" Jacob tried to peek at her screen.

She turned the phone off. "Just playing a game."

He sat beside her on the table under the shade of a tree. "No need to give me the cold shoulder. I'm being friendly." He bumped her knee. "Want to get more friendly?"

"I'm not looking right now."

Someone waved, her red costume fluttering in the slight breeze. "Jacob! And, hi, you must be the new Carla."

"I'm AJ."

"AJ, this is Amarilla, she plays the Scarlet Starlet. The good version of my Red Death," Jacob said.

Amarilla dropped beside her. "I've heard all the gossip about you. Now, give the good stuff." Her eager smile was slightly off-putting.

"What do you want?" Angela asked.

"Why are you here? Who are you with? How'd you get the job? All of it. Oh, and is it true you and Tyler Running Fox had a fling?"

Angela felt her cheeks heat with a blush. She brushed a strand of hair back from her eyes and began inventing wildly. "I, um, I'm from New York. I was... in a relationship, and things went bad. Really bad. So I decided a change of scenery and some time single was the cure. I came to LA, and voila! Here I am."

Amarilla leaned on the table. "Confirm or deny, you are The New York Girl?"

Angela frowned. "What do you mean The New York Girl?"

"Tyler left New York a few years ago," Jacob put in. "All the tabloids said it was because his one true love had spurned him for another man. Now you're here, a girl from New York, and rumor has it he was ignoring Glee for you."

"Oh! No!" Her blush deepened. "No. Um, no. Tyler and I, we, ah, we aren't... aren't anything, really. I think he hates me, actually. We're not friends. At all." She shook her head. "I'm not that girl."

Amarilla leaned in closer. "Who burned you in New York?"

"You probably wouldn't know him," Angela said. She tucked a stray hair behind her ear and tried to remember what Delilah's fictional history said she did. "I was on stage. Strictly chorus stuff, background frippery really. There was scenery with better billing than me."

"And the man behind the heartbreak?"

"Chris," Angela said without thinking. Chris Freeman and his temper were to blame.

Jacob whistled under his breath. "Wow."

"What?"

"Christian Sajemel and Tyler Running Fox were best friends before The Girl." Amarilla bumped her shoulder against Angela's. "I guess Christian's kinks weren't enough to keep you from Tyler's power-house." She winked.

"It's not like that at all!" Angela's face burned with more than the hot California sun. "Let's talk about something else. Jacob! Tell me about you. All about you."

Amarilla scooted closer to Angela. "He's named for a bed sheet."

Angela waited for one of them to start laughing. Neither did. "Okay. Now I want you to tell me she's lying."

"She's not," Jacob said. "My mom was a Twihard and obsessed with one of the characters."

"Tell her!" Amarilla urged, clapping. "It's gross!"

Jacob rolled his eyes and grinned in a sheepish way. "Promise to still go out with me after I tell you?" He hit her with a smoldering come-hither look.

Dark eyes? Check. Dark hair? Check. Shameless flirting? That was a new twist. "I didn't promise you a date at all."

He gasped dramatically. "I haven't won you over with my stunning physique yet?"

"Nope."

Jacob sighed. "If you must know, my mother's high school bedroom was decorated entirely with the face of a certain character from the Twilight series who shall remain nameless. I was conceived on sheets bearing his likeness."

"Ewww!" Angela laughed. "Wow."

"That's not the worst part." Amarilla poked Jacob. "Tell her the rest!"

"My mom kept the sheets, and my nursery had the same decorating scheme until I was thirteen." Jacob hissed through his teeth. "Yeah. It's embarrassing."

Angela and Amarilla fell into a fit of giggles.

"Jacob!" someone shouted from the studio's dark interior.

"And that's our cue to go wow them. Do you think you can toss your hair around in the wind?" Jacob asked, holding out a hand.

Angela hesitated.

Jacob stuck out his bottom lip in a pout. "No?"

"It's not you," she hurried to assure him. "It's... I was hurt, and I'm not ready to jump back in the ring." Not to mention that the chances of a rogue and a superhero finding true love were one in a million, and her parents had used that one chance up. On her way to the studio, she tossed her apple core in the outdoor compost bin. Jacob was a perfect Arktos she decided as she watched his movie-worthy rear end saunter off. But was it her imagination, or had he looked bulkier the night before?

She tried to remember being in his arms, the curve of his biceps blocking light and shrapnel from the explosion. Yup, definitely more mass. She'd have to tease him about padding his suit later.

There was a loud crunch behind her. Pivoting slowly, she scanned the empty courtyard. Not even a squirrel managed to get through studio security.

There was another crunch, like something small and warty eating an apple core out of boredom. She knew that sound. Leaning sideways ever so slowly she peeked behind the compost bin and saw the unholy offspring of a frog and a water balloon. It looked like an escapee from a kid's cartoon, a rounded squarish body with spindly arms and legs, bulbous eyes, all in eye-searing orange with blue polka dots. A second-generation minion.

Daddy had sent shock troops.

Of course he had. She grabbed the minion and squeezed. "How many of you are there?"

It tried to squirm out of her hand.

"Tell me, or you're confetti."

"Five!" the minion shouted. "Just five!" Its twiggy arms were surprisingly strong, or would have been if she hadn't been arm-wrestling minions since she was four for pennies.

Angela loosened her grip.

"Can I go now?"

"Oh, you're going all right." Straight back to Texas in the first box she could find. Her father was an excellent man in many ways, but he was a super villain and had been using minions since he was sixteen. Was there such a thing as rehab for minion abuse? *"Learn how to communicate without spies!"* or *"Six steps to not taking over the world and mowing the lawn yourself!"*

Not that she really wanted him to change, she assured herself as she snuck into the wardrobe room and dumped a two-thousand-dollar pair of black sandals onto the floor. It was just hard to maintain cover when hideous mini-monsters started stalking you on set. She stuffed the fussing minion in the shoe box with a sigh.

"AJ?" Jacob's voice filtered through the wall of the dressing room.

"I'll be right there!" She wrapped the box with a belt from the communal dressing table and shoved the minion in her locker to deal with later. The Hollywood promotional machine stopped for no man, woman, or minion.

* * *

Angela's eyeballs were fried. Hair billowing in the breeze sounded like a wonderful concept on paper, but the reality of staring into a fan with an open mouth and enough lip gloss to drown a goldfish wasn't a sexy one.

Jacob winked at her from his chair by the door.

"I thought you were done an hour ago," Angela said.

"I had time to wash the makeup off. Want to go get some dinner? There's this great little Greek restaurant on West Third that you'd love. The dolmades are to die for."

She scuffed her shoe on the cement floor of the studio. "I wish I could."

"But?"

"I'm still filling in as Glee's stunt double and there's another night shoot today. Tonight. Whatever." She rolled her eyes at her own rambling. "I need to take a quick shower and get down there. They still haven't found Glee's wig so I've been standing in for all sorts of random things."

"Why don't they just buy another wig?" Jacob asked as he picked up a black leather riding jacket.

Angela shrugged. "Search me."

He stepped close. "Is that an invitation?"

Angela's heart skipped as she remembered strong muscles cradling her. But she shook her head. "Not tonight." Or any other night. Not between them.

She risked opening herself up to catch his emotions. Frustration and excitement emanated from the next lot over, where Glee's action movie was filming. Jacob seemed quiet, although she caught a whiff of lust and dominance. Jacob brushed her arm with a finger. "I could wait for you to finish."

She stepped away. "That's sweet, but by the time I finish whatever it is I'm doing for Glee, I'm not going to be good company."

"Tomorrow night?"

"You're persistent, aren't you?"

Jacob crowded her again, his body heat making the small hall connecting the studio lots uncomfortably warm. "I always get what I want."

Angela's pulse quickened again, but this time it wasn't pleasant. "Good for you," she said, turning to walk away. "But I just left an abusive relationship and I'm enjoying some quality Me Time. When I'm interested in adding a man to my life, I'll give you a call." Angela left, walking just a little too fast, hoping the brush-off would be enough to cool Jacob down.

He caught up. "I don't get it. I'm good looking. I'm a nice guy. I'm the friendliest person you've met in LA. Why won't you have dinner with me?"

"Because I'm working two jobs, and I don't want to have dinner with anyone?" Angela shrugged. "This isn't about you. Relationships are a two-part harmony and if one part isn't playing along you can't have a relationship."

Jacob pursed his bright red lips, the remnants of the photo shoot giving him an almost clownish appearance. "I'm a nice guy, but I guess it's true what they say about nice guys finishing last."

Anger mounted. "Real Nice Guys don't pressure girls into dates, guilt-trip them over dumb things, or take someone saying that they don't want a relationship as a personal rejection. If you delivered pizza and I never asked for pizza, couldn't pay for pizza, and didn't want to eat pizza, would you be upset that I didn't take the pizza when you showed up?"

"Did you just compare sex to pizza?"

"Yes." She was practically running as she reached the door to the studio. The stage was set for another motorcycle scene and then some fancy dress party that Tyler was supposed to crash, probably with Glee in tow. Once again, Angela wondered if she could find a script. "Do you see Luiz?" The studio doors were open to the outside, a dingy alley with blue lighting bleeding into the sound stage with two sweeping staircases, a chandelier too glittery to be real, and the pompous air she expected from a library in a Disney movie. "Um..."

"Jacob!" Glee waved from her dressing room door. "Come here, baby!"

"See? She wants my pizza!" Jacob stuck his tongue out and then strutted toward Glee.

"Bless your heart," Angela muttered. Luiz's sharp whistle cut through the air. Angela turned around, looking for someone in black leather riding gear.

A hand tapped her shoulder. "Over here," Luiz said.

Angela frowned as she pivoted. Luiz was wearing a skimpy purple gown with a violent lime green stole. "That's not riding gear."

"The Talent are the only ones on bikes today. And Glee, of course." She snickered at her own joke. "The rest of us are playing Menacing Uninvited Guests at the museum party."

"Oh, the set is a museum?"

"You haven't read the script yet?"

"I keep meaning to do that."

Luiz pushed at her back. "Go get showered and into a makeup chair. And be grateful that they filmed the hot make-out scene already."

Angela shook her head as she retreated. "I really need a script."

CHAPTER EIGHT

Dear Mom,

I know normal people sometimes juggle two jobs, but I don't think they ever juggle two jobs like these. I spent all afternoon staring into burning hot lights with an industrial fan trying to whip my eyeballs out, took a thirty second shower, peeled myself out of the white banana suit, and pulled on a black silk negligee pretending to be haute couture.

I did finally get a script. Without breaking any confidentiality laws, I can firmly say that the writers watched way too many Indiana Jones and James Bond films in their youth. Ty is playing Indíbil Riberio, a Brazilian archeologist who is also an agent for Interpol. There's a criminal biker gang, a girl on the run from trouble, and more motorcycles than I ever needed to ride. Tonight's scene involves a bike wreck (onto very soft mats—I checked), a kissing scene in an alley (because Indíbil Riberio can't keep his hands off a semi-naked woman—at least that's believable), and then they break into the museum charity ball to steal the Thing! The

SHE SENT THE EMAIL as Tafi, the makeup artist, finished turning her into a stunningly edgy beauty her own mother wouldn't recognize. Angela tried standing in the boots wardrobe had provided. "I'm going to break my ankle if I run in these."

Tafi winced. "Boots? With this dress? Wanda? Why is the body double wearing boots?"

"No one will see her legs!" Someone, presumably Wanda, shouted from behind a row of gowns.

"Did you *see* the skirt? They're *supposed* to see her legs!"

Angela stood, tugging the dress down in an attempt to cover her panties. "My legs and everything else. This slit is indecently high." Apparently tonight's shoot called for wearing haute couture's sluttier cousin.

The stylist walked in, pink curls bouncing around bright red, cat-eye glasses. "Lose the panties. She needs to go commando. Find some strappy heels.

And somebody paint her toenails red. Glee has red nails. Her body double needs red nails. Think continuity people!"

Tafi gave a put-upon sigh. "Why isn't Glee doing this? I already did her makeup twice for this scene."

"She doesn't ride motorcycles," said the stylist.

"Or run in heels!" someone else shouted.

"Or film," muttered Tafi.

Angela wanted to lay her head down, but Tafi would kill her if she messed up a single curl before the shoot. Never mind that bullets would bounce off her shellacked hair. Tafi and Wanda held a quiet conversation. Fred, the shoes guy, was consulted. Finally Kerry, the lead stylist, was pulled in. Several black dresses that appeared identical to the one she was wearing were held up. She cringed when Tafi held up a strappy black nightmare left over from a BDSM shoot. At least haute couture's slutty cousin had a frill pretending to be a sleeve on the left side. It covered her stitches nicely.

Tafi returned with some strappy black shoes. "These cost more than I earn in a year. Do not break the heels."

"I'm going to break my ankle!"

"Ankles are replaceable. These are not."

Angela sighed mournfully. "I feel so loved."

Tafi shook her head. "Love is for headliners. You are a body double." She strapped Angela's shoes on. "Stand up. Turn. Good. You look like Glee."

"Which isn't the same as beautiful?" Angela guessed.

"You will look beautiful in the movie. Now. Go out there. Shake your shapely self. And pretend to be Glee so we can turn a profit on this. More profit means more rent money."

Angela rolled her eyes. "You're just my pimp, aren't you?"

"Work that money maker!" Tafi ordered as she pushed Angela to the set.

Blue filters covered the lights and Swendon's favorite smoke machines worked overtime to fill the false alley with fog. A motorcycle roared beside her. She jumped, then saw the crew playing with the sound effects panel. What she couldn't see was Swendon, Luiz, or whoever was working as Tyler's body double tonight.

She crossed her arms and waited for direction. A bright light flashed on, making the fog glow, and a motorcycle purred up beside her. The rider had a helmet in place. She smiled. "Let me guess, I need to come with you if I want to live?"

The rider's head shook slowly from side to side. "Get on," Tyler said, his voice muffled by the helmet.

"Why don't you have a stunt double?" She'd grabbed his waist just before he popped a wheelie and spun the bike around. "I hate you."

"Tyler? Tyler?" Swendon swam through the fog. "There you are. Mark, turn off two of those fog machines, this is too much. Okay. We've done the closeups already, but I need a good night shot of you racing away. AJ, do you see those green mats off on the right?”

She nodded.

“Good girl. When Tyler hits his mark, I want you to throw yourself at the mats. He’ll slow down enough for you to jump, but he won’t stop. Have you done something like this before?”

“Not dressed like this,” she said honestly.

“Don’t scuff the shoes. They’re expensive.”

She tightened her grip on Tyler’s waist as Swendon walked away. “I know I’m not as important as the shoes, but try not to kill me.”

Tyler revved the engine in response and tore down the alley, weaving between marks. As they drew near the mats, he jammed on the brakes.

Angela jumped, throwing herself at the mat and landing hard as she rolled. “Good times,” she muttered, climbing to her feet.

“You need to tuck and roll,” Luiz said as she held out a hand. “Get it right quick, or we’ll be shooting all night.”

“Right. Just like gymnastics.” She tried to remember the last time she’d jumped off a moving object to save her life. Probably when Blessing decided to drive and wanted to see if a car could fly. She’d thrown herself out of the car into the lake as her sister went off the edge of the pier. The car had flown fine, though the shocks hadn’t survived the landing. She walked back to the starting point.

Tyler pulled the bike up beside her. "Want a ride?"

"No. You like to throw me off your bike. Walking's much safer."

"Riding's quicker. Some of us need our beauty sleep."

"I hate to break it to you, Ty," she said, quirking an eyebrow, "but you'll never sleep enough to be pretty."

He gunned the engine and went to wait for her.

She climbed on and he was moving before she could grab his jacket. The bike slowed, barely, and she jumped. With a midair twist she managed a splashy landing on the mats and skidded across them.

"Perfect!" Swendon yelled. "Set up for the next shot. AJ, you're going to be in silhouette. Somebody show her the mark. Only one fog machine. Lights for the scene!"

The lights flickered, changing to illuminate a stretch of wall with a dozen cameras aimed at it. It was like being on the wrong end of the target range. Angela trudged over, leaned against the wall, and tried to ignore the throbbing in her arm.

Tafi dashed forward and fixed the hem of her dress.

Swendon wrinkled his nose. "AJ, try lifting a leg. Good, just like that. Now, breathe hard. You've just run from the bad guys, jumped off a bike, and you're alone and desperate and scared." Swendon clapped and turned to find other prey. "Tyler, stalk through the fog, throw the helmet to the side—not so hard this time—and go over to AJ. I need you to talk, we'll dub in the conversation we recorded this morning. Ready? Set? Action!"

Angela laid her head back on the fake brickwork, hoping it wouldn't crush Tafi's hard work. There should have been footsteps echoing. In the movies there always were. In reality, well, they probably added the sound effects after the filming. All she could hear was the sound of her own breath and the faintest whirring of cameras just past her elbow.

Fog swirled as a backlit hero approached. Pity it was Tyler. She watched him throw his helmet offstage towards the coffee pot. He swaggered toward her, all exaggerated gyrating hips and swinging shoulders. He stopped in front on her, leaned forward. The smell of mint toothpaste and his cologne filled the air between them. For a brief moment she regretted not putting on perfume. He was larger than life; she was a cowering mortal seeking safety.

"Talk!" Swendon screamed from deep in the fog. "Cut! We need lips moving! AJ, say something when he walks up, anything! No, nothing people will lip read easily. Again!"

This time she closed her eyes. Morpheus tempted her to the realm of Hypnos. Sleep...

Wonderful, promising, revitalizing sleep.

When she heard the helmet crash she lifted her head. Lips moving... "Would you like to play at questions?"

"How do you play that?" Tyler's voice was as deep and dark as his eyes. If he hadn't butchered *Hamlet,* she might have liked him.

"You have to ask a question."

"Statement." He put a hand on the wall beside her head and leaned in. "One–love."

She shivered in the cold air. "Cheating."

"How?"

"You always end in a Jade's Trick," she shot back, switching to Shakespeare because she couldn't remember the next line of Stoppard's play.

Tyler leaned closer, angling his head so his lips were a breath away. "I haven't started yet."

"I wonder that you're still talking, Signior Benedick. Nobody marks you."

His smile was devastating. It lit up the dark alley and promised to do wicked things until morning light.

Her pulse trilled and she knew she'd forgive him *Hamlet* if he kept smiling like that.

"What? My dear Lady Disdain? Are you yet living?"

"Is it possible Disdain should die while she hath such meet food to feed it as Signior Benedick? Courtesy itself must convert to disdain, if you come in her presence." Giving in to the invitation in his smile, she arched away from the wall.

Tyler rested his hand on her hip, urging her closer. "You and I are too wise to woo peaceably."

Lips near his ears, she whispered, "That's not the next line."

"Cut!"

Reality slammed back full force as Tyler turned away.

Angela stumbled back, gaping at the camera in shock. They'd been alone—at least, it had seemed that way.

Angela shook her head. Obviously the lack of sleep was causing hallucinations. There was no way she'd just zoned out and flirted with Tyler Running Fox, the butcher of *Hamlet*. Nope. Grandma Meredith would roll in all seven of her graves if that had happened. Proper Southern Ladies did not flirt with men who couldn't recite the 'To be or not to be' soliloquy correctly.

"Do you see that smile?" Swendon asked the world at large as he shook Tyler by the shoulders. "That will make us all very, very wealthy men. Why couldn't you smile like that earlier?"

Tyler held up a hand and chuckled.

Angela stared in horror. Heaven forfend, as Othello would say; he chuckled? He was human?

He hit her with another smile, warm, welcoming, the kind of smile that made panties drop. "AJ was seducing me with Shakespeare."

Swendon narrowed his eyes at her. "What?"

"We had a Shakespeare quote-off. I wasn't seducing him. I was... teasing." She nodded. That sounded believable.

A chorus of groans rose up from the cast. "Glee doesn't know Shakespeare," Swendon whined.

Angela smiled sweetly. "Sometimes I don't think Ty does either."

Tyler glowered down at her, but mirth danced deep in his dark brown eyes. "Let's reshoot the scene. I think someone wants to hear the 'To be...' speech from *Hamlet*."

"Done right," Angela confirmed, smirking.

"On your own time," Swendon said. He brushed Tyler's arm. "Where's special effects? Where's Yandel? Why does Tyler have blood on him in this scene?"

Tyler pulled his jacket off in confusion. "It's not mine. He glared at Angela. "Are you bleeding?"

"Um, I shouldn't be? I didn't have any of the special effects blood on me." But her arm hurt. She risked a quick glance. Blood seeped from under a torn stitch.

Tyler brushed her arm, his fingers cold on her pale skin. "What happened?"

"I must have popped a stitch out when I landed."

He motioned for Swendon. "Our stunt lady was improvising."

"AJ!" the director wailed. "Was any of that in the shot? It was such a perfect shot."

"Her arm was away from the camera," Tyler said quickly. He turned his attention back to her. "Why didn't you tell anyone you'd hurt yourself?"

"How did this happen?" Swendon demanded, pushing Tyler aside.

"I cut myself moving into the new apartment. I'm cleared for stunt work. Look, it's only a little blood. There isn't much. It just smeared. I'll pay to get the jacket cleaned if that helps."

Tyler shook his head. "You really are new to Hollywood. The Talent never pays for anything."

Angela glared back. "Then I guess I'm not The Talent. My parents taught me to take responsibility for my actions."

His eyes narrowed into angry slits. "Must be nice to have a couple grand to spend on a jacket."

"A couple grand?" Her voice squeaked.

"That's how much it will cost to replace the jacket." Tyler shrugged. "But you're a pretty white girl. I'm sure Daddy can pay for it. If not, there are plenty of people searching for their next porn star."

Angela rolled her eyes. "Grab a baby wipe from your Whine and Cheese bag, Running Fox. It's just a little blood."

CHAPTER NINE

Dear Mom,

Finding an all-night ER in L.A. isn't hard. I managed to get there and was only lost for, like, five minutes. Eight days in my new city and I've been to the ER! I think that's a family record of some kind. Do I get a trophy?

I'm okay. I ripped my stitches doing a stunt. It's not a big thing. I'm sore and exhausted, but hey, the Cupcake Shoppe was open when I drove past at four in the morning, so I grabbed one. With any luck, I'll be able to sleep until noon without interruption.

Your still tired daughter,
Angela

ARKTOS FOCUSED ON CHILLING the buildings around him so the pyro's fire wouldn't bring the block down and wished for approaching police sirens. This end of town was a victim of the last depression, home to nouveaux rich who had fled during the housing crisis, leaving empty buildings that had slowly filled again with vagrants. Though at least the street people were smart enough to run and hide when a flame-covered maniac attacked.

Another fireball blossomed in Arktos's face. He shot spines of ice at the pyro. The idiot capered backward, letting his heat melt the ice so he was merely splashed instead of skewered. Arktos tried throwing a cage of ice around him. It began steaming immediately.

Gravel crunched behind him.

Arktos pivoted and only instinct kept him from catching a baseball bat with his nose. It grazed his head, leaving his ears ringing. The blonde. Of course, he thought as he jumped to the side. He thought he'd been lucky finding the pyro alone.

Fire roared like a living beast, filling the alley behind him. He fought the fire with ice, but that only produced steam. He turned, trying to focus on putting up a thick glacier wall to cut the pyro out of the fight, and took a bat to the ribs for his inattention. They gave way under the force of the blow and he dropped to his knees.

The blonde swung again, slamming into the side of his knee.

Arktos swallowed a cry of pain and rolled to his back as he entombed himself in ice. He was a triple threat; able to fly, manipulate cold and ice, and heal rapidly, but he still needed time to heal in. If the blonde knocked him out, the pyro would turn him to a charred corpse before he could recover.

The fire outside his blue ice tomb dimmed. Two shadowy figures leaned over him and he felt heat on his back. Wiggling so he had some elbow room, he hit his knee, forcing the joint painfully back into place. He tried breathing and choked on blood. Broken rib. Wonderful. At least he'd be able to run in a few minutes.

His head spun as terror gripped him. This was it. He was going to die. Some dim corner of his mind shouted at him that this feeling wasn't his, that the terror was alien, but the fear flared higher, consuming the voice, consuming everything. He clawed at the ice, desperate to escape. He couldn't die like this. Wouldn't. Aaron needed him to come home.

A third person walked into sight. The ice distorted his view, warping the image so he could only see rippling lines, but even through the ice, he could make out the black and red costume—and the sudden drop in his terror levels—that had to mean Rage.

Arktos slammed his fist into the ice, punching his way free. She wasn't a triple threat and there was no way he was going to let some unprotected empath try to take down the pyro alone. He fought the pain and fear and ice until a swell of peace blanketed him.

Exhausted, he let his head drop back to the ground and saw the fleeing pyro burning bright as his ice cage melted away. "This was not the plan."

His ribs scorched. He turned to his good side and saw blood.

"Tell me about it. I hate having my beauty sleep interrupted." Rage bent over and picked up something silver that glittered in the pre-dawn light. "Cinderella left us a present."

She walked the battle lines looking for more loot before coming over to him and dropping to her haunches, dangling the silver earring above him. "Beautiful little trinket, isn't it? Silver or platinum, custom-made, expensive... I think I'll keep it."

Arktos winced as he tried to sit. "Give me the earring."

"I have contacts who can find out who made this and who bought it. I doubt you do. But, if you're very nice to me and keep talking, I might be persuaded to share my information."

He grinned through the stabbing pain in his side, panting only a little as bones shifted. "Are you going to scribble your phone number on my hand?"

She tossed the earring up, caught it in her gloved hand, and tucked it away in her pocket. "Do you know that little ice cream shop up on the Pacific Highway? The one near the overlook?"

Taking a shallow breath, he nodded.

"I like to drive up there at nights, watch the waves without the city all around me. I'll be there Friday. Maybe we can bump into each other, if you're out of the hospital."

"De nada. It's all good. I'm healing. Give me fifteen minutes and I'll only be sore." He reached out a hand. "Give me the earring."

"Not happening."

He coughed and winced again.

She raised an eyebrow. "That's a convincing impression of a pierced lung you're doing."

He smiled up at her. "For someone who missed her beauty sleep, you look great."

"And a concussion? Are there any other injuries I should tell the EMTs about when I call the ambulance?"

"Give me fifteen minutes." Arktos forced himself to sit upright, his muscles burning. "It'll hurt like hell, but I've had worse."

"When?"

"I was twelve..." He gasped and pressed his side. "I was twelve and my mom decided that taking a baseball bat to my head was a good way of reminding me how much she hated parenting me." Any other time he might have shrugged it off, but right now he couldn't work up the energy to move. "After lying on the floor overnight I woke up with a headache and the munchies. I blamed it on a bad dream until I saw the blood. This is better. I'll be hungry and sore, but that's it."

"Well, if I'd known this was just a midnight munchie run I would have brought cupcakes."

"I hate cupcakes. Your choices are either vanilla or chocolate and I hate both."

Rage leaned over him, crimson lips drawing his attention. "Blackberry-lime cupcakes."

Arktos chuckled, regretting it instantly as bone sawed at the muscles on his side. Definitely broken. "Why does 'blackberry-lime' sound like a pick-up line?"

"Because you're a male under age eighty. I could probably say 'antidisestablishmentarianism' and make you think about sex." She took his hand. "How about I stay here for a bit, just to make sure you recover enough to get yourself home."

"This isn't a death watch," he said through gritted teeth. Super healing. What a bad idea! Instead of letting a doctor pick out the organic shrapnel while he slept, his body pushed it out like an infection as new bone grew on the rib. His world narrowed to a point of shining light on the roofline where the first rays of dawn hit the metal trim. Pain swallowed him down into the darkness.

And then he felt suddenly light, like floating on a warm, lazy river, drifting away from the world.

"I'd worry less if you were talking," Rage prompted.

Arktos focused on the woman beside him. She was lovely, in a violent kind of way. The black leather trench coat had to be hot in sweltering L.A., but the humidity made her red silk cami cling in all the right places. Deep summer-sky eyes studied him intently. His hand shook. She'd come out here, alone, to save him. The pyro could have killed her—she had to have known it was a risk—but she'd still come to his rescue. The irony was enough to kill him.

He laced his fingers with hers. "What's your name?"

"What's yours?"

"You first."

Her smile turned seductive. "Statement. One–love."

He blinked.

"It's from *Rosencrantz And Guildenstern Are Dead*. The Question Game?" She waved her free hand airily. "At the university we made a game of reciting it to see who knew it best, but don't worry, most people don't know it."

"I know the play," he said. "I just don't expect beautiful women to start quoting Tom Stoppard at me instead of giving me their names."

"Ah. Well then." Her smile was wry, flirting but mischievous at the same time. He could get used to a smile like that.

"And I don't know the next line."

Rage grimaced. "I'm not sure I remember it either. Let me think." She muttered a few lines under breath, casually rubbing at her ribcage.

He tried to disentangle his hand when he realized what was happening. Rage could make people feel things, and she could feel other people's emotions, and now it seemed she could take some of it away.

The same pathways in the brain that registered emotion would respond to pain, wouldn't they?

"Let go," he whispered, not wanting to see her hurt. He tried harder to pull his hand away. "Stop it. I know what you're doing."

Rage arched a delicate eyebrow over her domino mask.

"You're taking—" The need to breathe cut him off.

"That's right." The pain ebbed away into nothingness. "I just took one year of your life away."

"Don't play the coy ingénue and quote *The Princess Bride* at me. You're going to kill yourself doing that."

"Kill myself by exciting your serotonin receptors? Somehow I doubt that."

"Empaths are like fire bugs, they can overload. Go insane. Burn out." He stared at the city lights reflecting off the smog overhead. "That's what's wrong with the pyro. He's about to burn out. If I can't get him in an isolation ward soon he will do his best impression of a firework and leave chunks of burned pyro all over the city."

"Graphic and unpleasant details that you should have mentioned sooner."

"Uh huh." He closed his eyes.

"Hey now! Stay with me here."

"Why?" He meant to ask why she was helping him but it was too hard to form the words. So easy to fall asleep.

Everything would be better tomorrow.

Her thumb caressed the sensitive skin on the palm of his hand. "Don't leave me. You're the only man who's made me laugh in years. You're kind."

"Says the woman who's known me for how long?"

"I can read emotions. It's there, all of it. Your worry for people, all the drives and concerns, all your insecurities. Simmering away just beneath the pain."

"Is that supposed to make me feel better?" he asked, voice rasping.

"What do you want to talk about?"

"Not me or my bare-naked emotions!"

"Do you want to talk about you being bare-naked?"

He opened an eye. Rage smirked, waggling her eyebrows in a suggestive way made famous by silent film. "No."

She sighed dramatically. "As you wish. Would you like to play at questions?" She held on tighter. "The next line is, 'What's your name when you're at home?'"

Arktos quit fighting. "What's yours?" Another cough shook him, but the pain was minimal.

"When I'm at home?"

"Is it different at home?"

"What home?" Rage shot him a triumphant smile that dared him to keep the game up as his muscles spasmed around the break.

Pushing himself into a sitting position, he asked, "Haven't you got one?"

"Why do you ask?" Rage stood and brushed dirt from her black jeans.

He stood too, wincing as he tested his knee. "What are you driving at?"

"What's your name?"

He smirked back. "Repetition. Two–love. Match point."

Rage stepped closer. "Who do you think you are?"

"Rhetoric. Game and match." He took her hand back. "A kiss for the winner?"

"I don't remember that part of the play."

"I'm improvising." Arktos brushed a stray hair back from her eyes. It felt like a wig, and the too-blue-to-be-true eyes were probably contacts. He couldn't bring himself to care. She'd been there to defend him. He traced her jaw line. "A kiss for the winner."

"Who won?"

"Does it matter?" he whispered, leaning forward. She met him halfway.

Arktos slid his free hand behind Rage's neck as she pressed against him. He ran his tongue across her lips and they parted, inviting him in.

Her hands rested on his shoulder, fingers kneading the muscle as she pulled him deeper into the kiss.

Arktos slid his hand under her jacket, feeling the sweat of the hot night and the thin layer of silk between him and her skin. He slanted his mouth, taking more. Demanding more.

She tasted of lime and vanilla, an exotic confection meant for him alone.

With a little gasp she pushed away. Her eyes were wide, her breath coming rapidly, cheeks flushed as if they'd done more than kiss. She shook her head to clear it, then came back to him.

Her kiss was desperate and raw, as though she could steal his soul and all the secrets of the universe with a touch of her lips.

Arktos leaned against the hot bricks behind him and lifted her, needing to feel the weight of her. Their tongues met again and this time he felt her control slip. It started as a strange warmth on his arms where skin touched skin, gliding over him until he was caught in a torrent of emotions. He felt her hunger for more, loneliness mixed with lust, desire warring with fear.

He pulled her tight against his chest in an attempt to comfort her. The need to protect her and drive away those fears was almost stronger than the need to know every inch of her. Almost.

But not here. They had to go somewhere quiet. Somewhere private. *Not home,* he thought as she bit his lip and slipped out of his hands.

Cold surrounded him as she withdrew. "Rage?" He held out a hand, inviting her back.

She stepped farther away, shaking her head. "No. No. It ends here."

"Ends?" He pushed away from the wall and pursued her. "What do you mean it ends here? It's only just started."

"This... Us? We are a bad idea. This can't happen." She wiped the back of her hand across her mouth. "We can't be together."

"I don't understand. Why not?"

She licked her lips, eyes drowning him with regret. "You can't give me what I want."

All the air left his lungs. *You aren't what I want.* His mother had used those words again, and again, and again. *Go away. I don't want you.* A rhythm as familiar as his own heartbeat. "What do you want?"

"A family. A husband, some kids, maybe not the white picket fence or a farm, but I want a family and you work for The Company. I can't be with you for the same reason I can't sign with them. I'd have to give up all I ever wanted, and I won't." She tugged at the edges of her trench coat, wrapping it around herself. "I'm sorry."

Arktos stared, trying to bring his defenses back up. "Kids? Isn't..." He took a deep breath, feeling his muscles mend and his heart break. "You know you can't, don't you? That's why it's part of The Company contracts. All superheroes are sterile. The same mutation that allows me to fly makes it so I can't father children."

She rolled her eyes. "What utter bunk."

"Bunk?"

"Southern Ladies don't swear."

She took a tentative step toward him, hand reaching out to caress his arm. "Superheroes can have babies."

He caught her hand and brought it to his mouth for a kiss. "I wish we could, but every one who's tried has died or been unable to conceive."

"That's not true."

"Do you have proof?" Every nerve was alive with the need to remove the space between them and kiss her again.

"I have proof."

Rage kissed him, and he tasted the salt of her tears. He let her go.

"My name is Angela. I'm the oldest of five children, and my daddy is a super villain."

CHAPTER TEN

Dear Mom,

What did Maria do? I've read your email twice and I think you let Gideon encrypt it because there's no way Maria has given up being the evil overlord of South America to work for the U.S. Forestry Service. Things like that don't happen in the rational world. Granted, my world has been less than rational lately, but that's because I gave up all pretense of having a brain and moved to California to work in Hollywood!

That came out wrong.

I'm happy here, really. Everyone is very friendly and the job isn't bad. There are worse jobs. I miss teaching. I miss feeling like I contributed something good to society. But I pay my rent and, for some reason, I have fans. I hope they're normal people and not... Well... Never mind. Least said soonest mended.

Your daughter who would prefer not to be a sex object,
Angela

SOME FLIGHT OF INSANITY had suggested that a run after Angela woke up would make everything better. Never mind the heat index of 105, or the ninety percent humidity, or the fact that she was supposed to be shooting night scenes for *Fractured* all week and should sleep until five.

No, she'd woken up at eleven and gone for a run.

At least the cop car that had been trailing her had finally turned off. The poor officer was probably worried that she was going to get heatstroke, which wasn't actually that farfetched an assumption, Angela thought as sweat dripped down her face. But half a mile ahead she could see the twinkling gem that was her destination: Cupcakes, a teeny tiny little building with a vacant lot next door that had been turned into an urban garden. It was the home of blackberry-lime cupcakes and worth the five mile run each way.

Angela put on one last burst of speed as 'I Am Not That Girl' by the Brutal Cheerleaders started. *I am not that girl. I can't be the one you want. I'll never fall that far. I am not that girl.*

Reaching Cupcakes, Angela paused to wipe the worst of the sweat off her face with her shirt, then opened the door and walked into the arctic chill of the bakery. The sharp contrast from the heat rose goosebumps on her skin, and tempting vanilla scented the air. It was a little piece of heaven, and for the moment it was all hers; the two small tables near the front window didn't exactly invite customers to linger. Angela pulled out her earbuds as the bell over the door jangled again. "A blackberry-lime and some water from the tap, please," Angela told the girl at the counter.

"Blackberry-lime and ice water," said a deep voice from behind her.

"Right." The girl stared past Angela, fingers suspended over the register.

Angela turned and looked up at Tyler Running Fox. He glanced at her and dismissed her without recognition. Angela suppressed an eye roll and turned back to the shop girl, still frozen in place. "Cupcakes?" Angela prompted.

"Uh huh." The girl blinked rapidly. "Is that Tyler Running Fox?"

"No, it's Harry Dresden," Angela snapped. "Can I have my cupcake, please?" She rubbed at the goosebumps that still prickled her arms.

"Sure." Abruptly, the girl remembered how to use the cash register and rang them up as the same order.

Angela tried to catch her eye to say something, but the girl was staring open-mouthed at Ty again. Grudgingly, Angela slapped a twenty down. "Keep the change." Not that there was much. They were not cheap cupcakes. She could probably make a batch for the price of one if she wanted to, but that would require complicated equipment like muffin tins and a citrus zester. Cookies were easier.

Tyler stood by the door, staring out the window but not seeming to look at anything in particular.

The area was full of tiny bookstores, art galleries, and eateries started by people with a bit of seed money and whole lot of dreams. It was hard to picture Tyler in that crowd. If he had dreams, they were the kind where he debated what country he wanted to buy when he filmed his next movie.

"Can I have my water?" Angela asked. The girl blushed and hurried away. Angela picked up the spare cupcake and walked over to Ty. "Here." From her earbuds the Brutal Cheerleaders crescendoed into the chorus: *I am not that girl. I am not the woman in your dreams. I am not the one holding on. I am not that girl.*

He glanced down at her with a frown.

She rubbed her arm again as she waited for him to match her face to the one he'd almost kissed on the movie set.

"Thanks." He nodded at her earbuds. "You've got good taste in music."

"Um, thanks." Angela wasn't sure what she'd been expecting. Maybe a, "Hi, AJ." Or a smile. Recognition, at least. Shaking it off, she grabbed her water and stepped back into the all-embracing warmth of the L.A. sunshine and smog. Heat kissed her skin.

Basking in the warmth, she sipped her water and devoured her cupcake. Angela tossed the wrapper into the little garden next to the shop, where the seeds pressed into the paper lining would become another round of cheerful, heat-resistant flowers. The orchids were her favorite.

After one last sip of water, she dumped the rest over her head and tossed the cup in the recycling bin. A stray thought tickled her senses; someone was watching her intently. She looked around, but saw only Ty, standing in the window, completely absorbed with nibbling at his cupcake. Weird.

By the time she arrived home her legs were shaking and the cupcake just a memory.

Mia and Aaron glanced up from the front step of the apartments where they were reading their textbooks. "Hey," Mia said. "How was your run?"

"Good." She sat down next to them. "Homework? Isn't school out yet?"

"Two more weeks," Mia said.

Aaron grumbled, "Finals."

"Can you help us? The teacher told us to read chapters seventeen and eighteen because they're on the final, but we haven't covered them in class yet."

"It makes no sense," Aaron said. "All I see are letters."

Angela nodded. "Yeah, let me get a quick shower."

"Real quick," Aaron pleaded. "My brother's coming in an hour."

She nodded again. "The fastest shower ever."

And it was. The water heater was broken for the third time this month but the pipes weren't well buried, so the water was still warm enough. She raked a brush through her wet hair, pulled on the first shirt and shorts she could find, and dashed back downstairs.

Mia giggled. "Nice shirt."

Angela glanced down at the white tee that had ZEPHYR GIRL emblazoned on it in sparkling blue letters. "What? It was my mom's. I like it."

"Help!" Aaron shoved his book at her. "What is this supposed to mean?"

They were still working on chapter seventeen when Aaron's brother roared up the street on his bike. Aaron groaned. "I gotta go. He has to work tonight. Can I come back for chapter eighteen? Please?"

"Yeah, I should be around this weekend." Angela smiled fondly at him and handed the book over. "Call Mia and she can get a hold of me."

Aaron shoved his books carelessly in his bag and put on his helmet. "Bye, Mia!"

"Bye!"

Aaron's brother waved too.

* * *

"Get a shower," Arktos said, tossing Aaron's bag against the wall. "I have work to do."

Aaron ran off upstairs as Arktos plucked old binders from the bookcase and piled them on the table. Every superhero started their career by inter-ning at the main offices on the east coast; he'd gone to NYU on their dime and worked at the offices scanning copies and filing paperwork in his free time. It would have been mind-numbing if the subject hadn't fascinated him: the whole history of superpower mutations had been collated in the four years he'd been there. He'd read about the first superpowers, about the heroes and the villains, about the ones that got away and the ones who were laid to rest in a quiet cemetery outside the city.

During his last semester, Katrina, the Company boss, made the move to a paperless office. He'd been in charge of shredding everything. The binders he retrieved now were filled with the papers that had escaped the purge, mostly original profiles handwritten by the heroes he'd always admired. He set the last of them on the table and flipped through the binder full of villains.

My daddy is a super villain.

Males and females alike stared back at him as he turned the pages. They weren't ugly, per se—the mutation seemed to grant good looks to most of them—but none looked like the kind of person you'd call 'Daddy.'

And then there was the other thing: most people didn't introduce themselves as the oldest unless they'd grown up with their siblings. Most. It was a gamble, but something about the way Rage had said it made him think she'd grown up in a nuclear family. That was her dream after all: mom, dad, the kids, maybe a dog.

The water shut off upstairs, and he considered her accusation that The Company was lying about children. Having Aaron around was already violating part of his contract. But what else was he supposed to do? Grandma could barely take care of herself, and Aaron was always getting into fights or ditching school. Moving him off the reservation to a private school in L.A. had made sense.

At least it had when he'd moved Aaron out two years ago. Since his little brother insisted on getting kicked out of every school in a thirty-mile radius, his prospects had dwindled to a single over-crowded public school on the poor end of town.

Aaron fit in perfectly. They'd grown up poor.

And letting him date Mia seemed to be a good choice so far. Mia was a level-headed kid and her tutor...

Arktos took a deep breath and rubbed his still-tender ribs. He'd almost driven straight past Mia's house because all he'd seen were long tan legs in too-short shorts. With her hair wet like she'd just stepped out of the shower, his mind had gone from brotherly concern for Aaron to tallying up his ten best pickup lines. And then swung straight to guilt, because he was mentally cheating on Rage, who didn't want him anyway.

He leaned his head back. The stuccoed ceiling offered no inspiration for his women troubles. Beautiful blondes; there were two too many in his life right now.

Forcing the memory of Rage's kiss from his mind, he opened the second binder, full of the forgotten ones. The super villains who got away, the superheroes who went rogue, all the people who had dropped off the radar for whatever reason.

Most of them weren't even in the computer system. No one had felt the need to file the cold cases. But some of them were promising: at the very back of the binder was a model photo, a handsome man in a three-piece suit who was smiling at the camera like his career depended on how many people swooned. At the bottom of the same page, Arktos had tucked an old print photograph of a blonde woman with a warm smile and the words ZEPHYR GIRL printed across her white shirt in metallic blue.

He took the photograph out and set it to the side. Doctor Charm and Zephyr Girl were in the wrong folder. They were both dead, killed in an explosion at Doctor Charm's lab during a fight.

The smile on Doctor Charm's face drew his attention, though. Rage had the same chin, a similar bone structure. And Charm was the sort of villain someone would take as a lover, too.

"Hey," Aaron said as he headed for the fridge. "What's for dinner?"

"What are you making?"

"A sandwich." Aaron stopped to look over his shoulder. "Nice job, big brother. Did you get her phone number?"

Arktos's forehead crinkled in confusion. "Whose?"

"Angela's." Aaron reached down to grab Zephyr Girl's photo. At Arktos's stumped expression, Aaron wiggled the picture. "Mia's tutor? The hot chick teaching me math? The one with the legs you were staring at?"

Arktos colored and snatched the photograph away. "That's Zephyr Girl."

"Really?" Aaron shrugged. "Then AJ is her clone. Barbie doesn't have outfits that match that perfectly."

Arktos looked at it again. "Rage said her name was Angela, and that her father was a super villain," he told Aaron as the pieces slowly fell into place.

"Did she mention her mom was a superhero? That's the sort of thing I'd mention."

Arktos flipped the pages to check the death dates of the hero and villain. "Go upstairs. Get the blue book in my closet, the big one."

"Okay." Aaron gave him a long, critical look.

"Hurry!"

Aaron ran and came back with the book. "What's in here?"

"Superhero missions. It's one of the books Katrina wanted tossed because of water damage, but I managed to find somebody who could redo the binding. Check page ninety-two, I think that's it. Operation Poisoned Apple."

"Sounds cheerful," Aaron said as he sat and turned the pages. "Here it is." He slid the binder across the table.

Arktos studied the photographs. "What's it say?"

"Ah, not much, it's a summary of an operation that was busted. Some heroes went rogue and wanted to kill the kids of super villains, but it was busted up by some heroes. Um, why can super villains have kids if you can't?"

Arktos pressed his lips together. "Good question. Are there any names?"

"Rolling Shock. The Rainbow Dane." Aaron chuckled. "Oh, here, Zephyr Girl; she's the one who broke the ring up after going undercover as a rogue."

"Year?"

"Twenty-twelve."

Arktos's heart skipped. What did this mean? He held the photograph out to his brother and caught his gaze. "Aaron," he said slowly. "Zephyr Girl died. In 2005."

CHAPTER ELEVEN

Dear Mom,

I'm trying to picture Maria joining the U.S. Forestry Service and I'm drawing a blank. The mind boggles.

By the way, do you have Delilah's work number? I asked her to look into something for me and she's refusing to answer her cell phone. I need to talk to her ASAP.

Love,
Angela

THE APARTMENT WASN'T MEANT for pacing, but Angela tried anyway. Five steps to one corner, six steps to the next—three if she didn't want to go into the kitchen—five, six... "Delilah, pick up your phone!" Picturing her sister diving for the ringing cell didn't do any good. Delilah's playback tune circled around for its second replay, because everyone wanted to spend their night listening to orchestral arrangements.

"Hello?"

Angela squeezed the phone. "Delilah! Where have you been?"

"At work."

Angela checked the clock. "Isn't it a little late for work?"

"I had to go back to the office after a funeral." Delilah sighed on the other end of the line. "Is someone going to die if I ask you to call back next week?"

"Maybe."

Delilah paused. "Someone we like?"

Angela bit her lip. "Yes?"

"Angela, what are you doing over there? I thought you were supposed to be lying low and keeping out of trouble."

"I'm not in trouble. I'm observing trouble. There's a big difference." She resumed pacing. "There's... It's complicated. I'm sorry. Whose funeral were you at?"

"Midwestern Fury's; he was the main superhero for Chicago."

"And you killed him?"

"No. I went to his funeral to see if I could find his killer. He's the second superhero we've lost this year."

Angela checked the phone to make sure she had the right number. "Why do you care? I thought you were firmly anti-hero."

"I am, but the same big game hunters who go after superheroes like to hunt my big name clients. I told you about that stalking case back in February. I think it's the same person, or the same group. Atlanta's Golden Hunt is the name the man gave me, but I still don't have enough evidence to hand the case over to the police and get them shut down."

"They hunt humans?"

"Just apex predators in general, but to join they need to kill a human, yes." In the background Angela could hear the soft clicking of a keyboard. "The stalker and I had a good chat before the police arrived. All right, I have your data. The earrings are custom work made by Jorge Fidel out of Brooklyn. He made two sets of twisted silver and platinum— good call on that. One set is still in the Brooklyn showroom, the other was sold to Tyler Running Fox. According to the gossip, he gave them to his girl-friend."

"Ty doesn't have a girlfriend," Angela blurted out. She rolled her eyes at herself and continued. "At least not that anyone's mentioned to me."

"Glee Keni? The actress?" Delilah made an exasperated sound. "Why am I the one who knows who's dating who in Hollywood when you're the one who lives there?"

Angela shrugged and readjusted the phone. "I've worked on set with both of them. If they're dating then it's a low-key relationship."

Delilah snorted. "Wishful thinking, kiddo. In the past month, a man acting as Running Fox's agent has purchased close to a million in jewelry for Glee. Rings, necklaces, lots of bracelets." More clicking followed. "Hmmm. Does Running Fox have a gambling problem?"

"Not that I'm aware of, why?"

"His net worth is a fraction of what it should be. Let me check... Good grief. He spends an estimated ninety percent of his income on charity. That's ridiculous."

"Ten percent of his income is probably more than normal people earn in ten years." Angela flopped on her couch. "So, I guess that confirms most of my worst fears."

"Oh? Am I missing some sisterly gossip?"

Angela mumbled under her breath, and then with a sigh, told her sister about the pyro and Arktos. "Both are familiar. I knew I'd bumped into them before, but this just makes it worse. The blonde dropped the earring. She and Pyro are close. I guess it makes sense that it's Glee and Tyler. And Jacob told me when we first met that he was a superhero."

"You don't sound certain."

"Jacob... He's nice. I guess. I don't know. He gives off a weird vibe sometimes. Very possessive. Very controlling. Arktos isn't like that."

"It could be that he feels like a different person in uniform. Or maybe Jacob is a superhero but isn't Arktos. Either way, you need to stay away from them."

"I know." She crossed her arms. "I told Arktos it wouldn't work. That we couldn't... anything, really."

"Good, because you can't. Not without blowing your cover sky high. He's Company, Angela. They're monsters."

She rolled her eyes. "One day that attitude is going to get you into trouble. No," she said over her sister's protest. "Skip it. What about Travys? Have you found out anything about him?"

"He's buried deep. The case never made it to public records. I'll work on it tonight after I go over the data I collected from the funeral."

"Delilah, this Golden Hunt thing. Don't try to attract their attention. Okay?"

"Would I do something like that?" Delilah asked with an air of innocence.

"Yes."

"Meh. I'll be careful. I'm collecting data in my role as a security advisor. I'll let the police handle everything. I'll call you when I have something on Travys."

"Okay. Love ya. Bye."

"Bye."

Angela stared at the silent phone. It took her a moment to realize she was holding her breath. She shivered as she forced herself to draw oxygen into her lungs. Poor Travys. Poor her. Why couldn't The Company just leave her alone? All she wanted was a normal life: a job, PTA meetings, maybe someone to go to the movies with on a Friday night.

There was a knock at the door before it swung open. "AJ, you need to lock up. This is L.A.," Luiz said as she walked in. "What are you doing?"

"Um." Angela waved the phone. "Waiting for a phone call and moping."

Luiz's forehead wrinkled. "Is everything okay?"

"Yeah. I guess. It's just... family stuff." Angela shoved her phone under the couch pillow. "What do you need?"

"Mia's school is holding a fundraiser tonight at the Salsa Bar. The whole charter school funding thing. I'm trying to drum up some support." Luiz did a quick rumba step. "Want to go dance?"

"Sure. I..." Well, why not? It was better than moping. "Yeah. Sure. How much is it?"

"Twenty-five will get you in, but all donations go to the school fund so they can buy the old building. If they can get enough by July first they can open the school after Labor Day in September." Luiz gave her a cheesy grin. "How's that for a sales pitch."

Angela smiled back. "I'll grab some cash."

"Great! I'm going to go knock on some more doors. I put flyers up at the studio but the Salsa Bar is the low-rent district and I don't think we're going to get a great turnout."

"I promise to put on something pretty and flirt with anyone who makes eye contact as I drive over. With my helmet on. Visor down."

Luiz rolled her eyes. "Very helpful. Thank you."

Angela retrieved her phone and went to raid her closet for dancing clothes. She didn't own much in the way of flirty, super-short skirts, and she wasn't going to wear a skirt on her bike anyway. Instead she grabbed tight white jeans and a shimmering blue blouse with an asymmetrical hem. If the party got really hot she could kick off the jeans and just wear the shirt as a super-short dress. She pulled it on and did a practice turn in the mirror. It covered all the important bits. Good enough.

It took thirty-five minutes to work her way through L.A. traffic to the little shack on the beach that served up Latin dance music, south-of-the-border food, and the best selection of homemade salsa in the state of California. Angela found herself checking her side mirrors the whole way, watching for a familiar black bike. But if Arktos was out tonight, he wasn't on her side of town.

Which was good, she reminded herself. They'd kissed. That was it. It was time to laugh it off and move on.

Angela parked her bike at the end of a long row, trying to make sure she wouldn't get boxed in. Mia was on door duty, smiling winningly with the line of people dropping twenties into her cash box and flirting with Aaron, who sat beside her with a proprietary air.

Mia waved when she saw Angela. "Hey! I wasn't sure you were coming."

Angela smiled. "I wasn't, but your mom dragged me out of the house. How's the fundraising going?"

Aaron grimaced and Mia's smile turned brittle. "It could be better."

Angela fished an envelope filled with cash out of her pocket. "Here, see if that helps."

Mia started counting. "Holy mother of... AJ! Where did you get this?"

Aaron took the envelope from Mia and counted. "Did you kill somebody?"

"My sister sent me some cash to help me set up a new house. I figured I have a job. I don't need handouts."

"What does your sister do?" Mia asked.

Angela looked at the envelope filled with money taken off drug runners when Maria had taken over South America. "She's in law enforcement."

"I'm going to be a cop when I grow up," Aaron announced. "This is bank."

"Will it help?"

Mia nodded eagerly. "This gets us a lot closer. Thank you." Salsa music wafted out into the sultry evening air.

"You should go dance," Aaron said, nodding toward the door. "My brother's in there complaining because no one knows how to tango.”

Angela laughed. “And I’m supposed to find him how? Is he wearing his helmet?”

“Can you tango?” Aaron asked.

“I learned in college. There was a competitive dance team. It was basic stuff, but it was fun.”

“Go inside!” Mia ordered. “No one’s dancing. It’s worse than a freshman social.”

“I’ll tell my brother to come say hi to you!” Aaron called after her.

As soon as she opened the door, Angela was hit by the savoury smell of grilling meat and hot chiles. All the tables had been pushed to the side to open up the dance floor, but everyone was avoiding it. Shrugging off her riding jacket, Angela worked her way through the crowd, searching for Luiz.

“AJ!” Luiz’s hand waved over heads. “Over here!”

“Hey,” Angela said as she pushed her way to the bar past a group of men arguing the baseball season. “You’ve got a good turnout.”

“Everyone’s paying minimum cover,” Luiz said. “The Salsa Bar takes five per head, plus the cost of food, so five people make a hundred dollars.”

Angela did a quick head count. “You’re going to need another fundraiser.”

“Don’t I know it!” Luiz took her drinks from the bartender and paid him. “We staked out a table over in the corner. Here, take this.” She shoved a pink drink into Angela’s hand and led the way.

A tall Latino man met them halfway and took the drinks. "AJ," said Luiz, "This is my brother, Miguel. Miguel, AJ David."

He set the drinks down on a table and held out a hand. "My friends call me Mikey, but you can call me Lover."

Angela shook his hand, and he pulled her toward the table. She pushed back. "Thanks, but Mikey is fine. I'm not in the market for a boyfriend right now."

"Who said anything about dating?" Mikey asked as he let her go and opened a beer. "I just want to give you a proper L.A. welcome."

Luiz smacked him upside the head. "Ignore him," she told Angela. "And you," she said, rounding on her brother, "no more beers. You're in enough trouble."

"It's just one!" Mikey protested. "I'm not driving! Let me relax."

Ignoring the bickering siblings, Angela scanned the room for familiar faces. Jacob was on the far side of the room. He held up a drink when she caught his eye and winked at her. She waved. So. He really was a superhero after all. That was... weird. She tried to picture kissing Jacob. It didn't work. Arktos? No problem, she dreamt about that, but superimposing Jacob over Arktos's mask still felt wrong.

"Mikey!" Tyler Running Fox caught her off-guard and she almost stepped on his foot when she turned. "Luiz. AJ. How's things?"

"Hey, Tyler," Luiz said as Angela slid out of the way. "I didn't expect to see you here."

He shrugged. "I saw the flyers and thought I'd help."

"Tyler!" Mikey raised his beer. "How is my favorite stunt face?"

Tyler chuckled. "I'm good. I've missed having you on set though."

"I bet you did," Mikey said. "Who was riding for you?"

"I did my own stunts while you were gone. It wasn't a big thing." Ty's gaze slipped her way and Angela shrunk back, bumping the wall with her shoulder blades.

Mikey took the opportunity to grab her hand. "What do you think, sweet thing? Would you rather go riding with me or Tyler here?"

"Um." Angela licked her lips and tried to find a polite reply. The room was too crowded. There were too many emotions and too many thoughts, too many people sizing her up like a prize cow at the auction. Pyro. She struggled not to say it aloud as she forced the tangled emotions aside.

"AJ's been riding with me all week," Tyler said. "Consider it the perks of staying sober and employed." He picked a pretzel out of Luiz's bowl with a smile.

"Luiz!" Angela said, desperate to escape. "Do you dance?"

"Not if I can avoid it," Luiz said as another tango began.

On the other side of the room she could see Jacob eying her. The music was getting louder; all she wanted to do was run out, jump on her bike, and get as far away from L.A. and superheroes as ten bucks' worth of gas could get her.

"I dance," Ty said.

She turned, stunned. "Really?"

"Do you want to?" He held out his hand, waiting for her, not demanding anything.

Angela let her boundaries slip a little, trying to sort through all the emotions in the room. *Come on,* she told herself. *You can do this. This is small fry.* She found Tyler's emotions. He was calm, almost disinterested. She could turn him down or dance with him; neither would change what he thought about her. "Sure," she said, taking his hand lightly as her pulse evened. "Let's dance."

They stepped onto the dance floor as the tempo picked up and Ty moved away from her, circling back, a predator on the hunt. There was no choreography for this, only instinct. A tango was a primal dance, an expression of desires as old as time.

Angela shivered in the air-conditioned spotlight. A dance. It was just a dance. Taking Tyler's hand she moved with the music, a few basic steps. A twist. A dip. And then she was pressed against him, feeling the warmth of his hand on her back, the scent of his sandalwood cologne overwhelming the distant smell of the grill. The pyro hadn't smelled of sandalwood.

Angela pushed him away, moved into a more complicated series of steps that was meant to flare a skirt but still got her point across in jeans.

Tyler followed, his smile predatory. He caught her, pulled her back to him.

She gave him a sultry stare as she lifted her foot and caressed the length of his leg. *So. It's like that, is it.*

He dipped her, turning her in time to the music, and pulling her back up.

They promenaded, walking together as the music crescendoed. Tyler led her into a series of tight turns, a split, and then a final dip as her heart raced and the music came to an end. His hand slid down the length of her body, resting for a second longer than was kosher on her rear, and then he pulled her out of the dip with a wink.

Angela managed a weak smile before she retreated to the heat and darkness off the dance floor.

Luiz had both her eyebrows up. "Where did you learn to dance?"

Angela snatched up a bottle of water. "College."

Luiz shook her head in awe. "Girlfriend, that was scorching. If I weren't one hundred percent het, I'd make a play for you."

Angela scowled as she uncapped the bottle. "Try Ty."

"Nope. Still too much like my ex." Luiz grinned.

"I'm het," Mikey said, eyes hungry with lust. "Come with me. Have my babies." He dropped out of the chair onto one knee. "Marry me!"

Angela took a slug of water. "No."

"Hey, AJ." Warm arms slipped around her. "That was sexy," Jacob whispered in her ear.

"Thanks, I—" Her phone rang and she edged Jacob aside so she could pull it out of her back pocket. Delilah's number lit up the screen. Her chest tightened. "I've got to take this. Family stuff." She waved to Luiz as she hit the answer button.

"I've got bad news for you," Delilah said without preamble. "I found Travys."

CHAPTER TWELVE

Dear Mom,

Delilah found Travys, the boy who shot me. He's in jail on murder charges. There wasn't a trial. There couldn't have been a trial. I'm not dead, so he can't be guilty of anything. But The Company has something on the judge.

It's a trap. If I go back to rescue Travys I'll have to go to court, prove I'm alive, and disprove everything The Company will say about me. I checked my old TalkPlace account. All the teachers from the school have unliked me. I did a little social media stalking on RealTime, and they all think I'm a pedophile. The Company convinced them that Travys shot me because I hurt him.

I want to hurt somebody. I want to make them feel the way I feel right now. I want...

I want it all to have never happened. I want to be back at school, planning my final exams and my touristy attack on New York. I was going to go to Broadway. I was going to see my kids graduate and help them finalize their college applications. I was going to do something other than run around in a trashy plastic suit pretending to be a slutty version of you.

I want to do something good; instead I'm stuck in a cheap cosplay so Geoff Swendon can relive his adolescent fantasies.

I miss teaching. I miss being me.

Angela

"DO YOU KNOW HOW hot you are?" Jacob asked, wrapping his arms around Angela from behind as she stepped off the set. "I could just eat you up."

"Ugh." Angela tried to shrug him off as Jacob nuzzled her neck. The plastic suit she wore as Pacifica clung to her sweaty body. "I'm melting in this heat. Seriously, I'm disgusting. Let me get a shower."

He held her tighter. "Who were you texting?"

"It was an email to my mom. Please, let go." She pushed his hand away.

Jacob stepped back, arms wide. "What?" he sneered. "Holding out for Running Fox? You think he'll get your name on the A-list?"

Most of the film crew stopped to watch them.

"What are you talking about?" Angela demanded in a whisper. The crew was breaking things down for the night and after the day's tabloid headlines, the last thing she needed was a fight.

Jacob scowled. "I saw you dancing with him. You like him more than me!"

"News flash, Jake," Angela said, tossing her hair. "I'd be the same if I were dancing with Quasimodo! It's a tango. It's supposed to look like an erotic argument."

He frowned. "You liked it."

"I like dancing. That's not a crime."

"It should be the way you do it." He pouted, then tilted his head to hit her with a dark-eyed smolder. "Don't be mad. I'm just jealous. Running Fox has it all. The girls, the gigs, the money... I don't want to lose you to him. That's not fair." He held out his hand.

"You can't lose me," she said in prelude to explaining that he didn't own her, but the director walked past. "Give me a sec, Jake. Mr. Swendon!" She chased him down.

Geoff Swendon turned midstride. "AJ, sorry about the AC. They'll have it fixed by tomorrow. Thanks for being such a trouper out there."

"Can I talk with you for a minute?"

He checked his watch. "I can give you ninety seconds if you talk fast."

"Alone, please. It's about the finale."

The director went pale. "Ah..."

Angela nudged him into compliance.

"Step into my office," he muttered. "At least I have a fan in there."

It was a ramshackle little space that looked like a secondary prop room, but it fit Geoff. He collapsed into a worn, patched chair with a sigh. "I'm not killing Pacifica," he said without preamble. "The writers tossed the idea around, but everyone likes you. We won't kill you."

"I want to die!"

Geoff blinked at her and she blushed.

"I mean, I think Pacifica needs to die. It fits her character. She would sacrifice herself, and the weapon you plan to use, she's the only one who could get close. Who else would sacrifice themselves to save a villain's life?"

"Are you trying to talk yourself out of a job?"

Angela shifted awkwardly. "It fits. And I'd feel guilty if someone else left. You brought me in on a short contract to fill in for Carla. Everyone else has worked so much harder."

The director started laughing. He slapped the table. "Wow!" Wiping tears of mirth from his eyes he grew serious. "Who put you up to that little speech?"

"No one."

"Come on. Tell Poppa Swendon the truth. Little girls with Hollywood dreams don't throw it all away over a guilt trip."

Angela racked her brain for an excuse he'd accept. "I'm scared."

"Of what?"

"People." She grimaced. "Red carpets, award shows, the hordes of people. I... I just... It makes me nervous."

"Didn't you act on Broadway?"

"Only in the chorus. No one knew me. I never had to go to photo calls. I was anonymous. The idea of walking the red carpet gives me panic attacks." She forced a tear. "Please? Kill off Pacifica."

He swiveled back and forth in his chair. "I'll think about it. No promises. But you still need to be at the dinner Friday night."

"What dinner?"

"Call Jacob in here," Swendon ordered. "I know he's lurking out there."

Angela brought Jacob in and took up as much of the precious air space in front of the fan as she dared.

"Jacob, I need you to promise to stay with AJ on Friday night. She's panicking over her first red carpet."

"Happy to, sir," Jacob said as he slid an arm around her waist and pulled her in for a tight hug.

The room really was too stuffy for three people. Jacob hugging her in her sweaty suit was going to give her heat stroke.

Angela shifted away and raised a hand. "What's happening Friday?"

"The studio head's birthday blowout in New York," Swendon said. "It's the biggest party all month. Two red carpets, one for the dinner and one for the actual party."

Angela's knees buckled.

Jacob caught her. "Easy there, Peach. Don't go fainting on us."

"It's this costume. I need to change into something cooler." She plucked at her collar. "I can't go to New York on Friday."

"Why not?" Jacob asked. "Do you have a hot date?" He raised his eyebrow, daring her to admit she had something planned.

"Yes. A very hot date with a very cool guy."

Jacob kissed her on the forehead and winked. "Don't worry. I'll be there."

CHAPTER THIRTEEN

Dear Mom,

I have no idea why Delilah would say she couldn't meet you for dinner this week. That's weird. Maybe there's a man in her life.

Your single daughter,
Angela

"DELILAH, I'M SERIOUS. WHAT am I supposed to wear to this thing?" Angela asked as she dropped the pile of clothes next to her suitcase. The ancient apartment's air conditioning wheezed as it fought the heat wave. Last night she'd opened the window out of desperation, hoping to catch a night breeze, but she was still sweating.

"You need a conservative suit."

"A what?"

There was a pointed silence from the other end of the line. "Please tell me you're joking. Don't you own any business clothes?"

Angela held up a vintage Marchesa dress borrowed from her mother. The light caught on the gold leaf hidden under wispy, ocean-blue gauze. "Hollywood and Chicago have very different standards."

"I'll bring you something." Delilah said something away from the phone and then came back. "I've found the video The Company is using to blackmail the judge. It's bad. Career-ruining bad."

"Can you handle it?"

"I'm trying to see if I can make it vanish. If they have it locked down at Langley I can't waltz in and grab it. The Company headquarters are a different matter."

Angela held up another dress, this one a rich purple with strips of gem-encrusted illusion netting. It would make her look like a high-priced hooker, but it would work. "I thought you'd been to Langley."

"On official business as a guest, yes. Not after hours. They have pretty good security."

"Pretty good?"

"They aren't my level of good, but so very few people are. I have a black suit that should fit you. Do you own a blouse?"

"A what?" She tossed two sets of jeans into the carry-on and tried zipping it. Too much. Her jeans might have to stay home.

"I'll find you a blouse. No jewelry. No perfume. Can you do that?"

"Why would I be wearing either?" The zipper finally closed on her bulging bag.

"Sometimes I find it difficult to believe we're related."

Angela fell backwards on her bed. "I got Mom's genes, you got Grandma Meredith's."

"Ewww!" Delilah squealed. "That's a horrible thing to say to someone! I am not anything like her. I'm like Daddy, I enjoy the finer things in life." Something rustled in the background. "Who's the guy from the tabloids? Is that really Tyler Running Fox? Jeans? Did you really wear jeans to go dancing?"

"I rode my bike there!"

"Doesn't L.A. have cabs?"

"It doesn't matter. I didn't intend to dance. Yes, that's Ty. No, we are not in a relationship. No, there is no chance of us being in a relationship. No, I didn't enjoy dancing with him."

"Liar. He is so your type."

"Shut up." A motorcycle roared on the street below. "I gotta go. My ride to the airport is here."

"Okay, I'll see you tonight. Get to the back door of the center by nine and I'll pick you up."

Angela picked up her discarded jeans and shimmied into them. "You realize how hard it's going to be to break away, right?" she asked as a piece of paper drifted to the floor.

"Make it happen. Love you." Delilah hung up.

Sometimes having a Type A personality sister was a real pain in the B. She picked up the scrap and unfolded it.

FRIDAY 11PM—I'LL FIND YOU

Downstairs Luiz honked the horn. Who was she meeting tonight? Besides Arktos, who she wasn't meeting because she'd be in the wrong state. She took the stairs two at a time trying to think of names. She hadn't worn the jeans to work, just dancing...

The memory of Tyler's hand fondling her brought a cold flush to her skin. A hot dance. His fingers caressing a part of her body they had no business touching. The wink as he walked away.

Damn. He probably thought she'd check her pocket as soon as she left the dance floor.

"Hey, AJ," Aaron said as he passed her on the stairs.

She shook herself back to the moment. "Hey." Aaron was headed for the bike. "Where's Luiz?"

"She and Mikey left a couple minutes ago," Aaron said as he reached for his helmet. "They had to stop and see his parole officer before they went to the airport."

Angela checked the time on her phone. "I guess I'll have to pay for parking. There's no way she's going to make it back in time to give me a ride. Dang it."

"I can give you a ride," Aaron's brother said, his voice muffled by the helmet.

"Oh?" She blushed. "It's okay. You need to get him home. I'll be fine, thanks."

"It's no problem!" Aaron rushed to say. He practically threw the helmet at her. "You go. I'll go study with Mia some more."

Angela wagged a finger. "Uh uh. Luiz would flip out if you were here without adult supervision."

"We'll sit on the front steps. Promise. It only takes an hour or so to get to the airport and back. We'll be good."

Aaron's brother sat on the bike contributing absolutely no support for her arguments. "I don't know."

"Please?" Aaron begged.

"If anything happens, I will help Luiz bury your body," Angela warned.

"You're losing plausible deniability," Aaron's brother said. "Hop on. We'll call it payback for the tutoring."

"Payment," Angela corrected automatically. "Payment is when you reimburse someone for services rendered. Payback is when you get even with them."

He held out a hand. "Payback, because when you tutor my brother I spend the whole time racking my brain for a decent pickup line. You always leave me tongue-tied."

"Have you come up with a good one yet?"

"Not yet."

"Try two tickets to the Shakespeare festival next month. They're doing *Much Ado About Nothing*." She put on the helmet and climbed on the back of the bike, her clothes secured in her suitcase-slash-backpack.

"And wilt thou have me?" Over the helmet intercom his voice still sounded muffled, but she detected a note of Aaron in there. When the kid's voice dropped another octave he'd probably be a double of his big brother.

"Aye, and twenty such."

"I'm a unique man. You might have to settle for just me." He switched lanes. "That's all you need for a weekend getaway?"

"I hope it's two dresses too much." She wrapped her arms around his waist as they coasted down the street. "Why can't people wear jeans to parties?"

"Not fancy enough," he said as they merged onto the highway.

She leaned her head down, trying not to look at the traffic all around them. "I hate not driving myself."

"You should have said something earlier." He chuckled.

It was a soothing sound. The bike was moving fast enough to create a breeze and for the first time in days she felt her skin prickle into goosebumps. Angela sighed happily.

"You're supposed to hold on."

"I am holding on."

"Hold me tighter."

She did, and they made record time to the airport.

Aaron's brother pulled up to the curb. "So, we have a date next month?"

"Do you have tickets?"

"I can have them. You'll go even though you've never seen me?" He shifted nervously in his seat. "I mean... You know."

"Aaron talks you up a lot, but if it makes you feel better, we can go as just friends." She held the spare helmet out. "Thanks for the ride."

"AJ?"

"Hmmm?"

"What if I want us to be more than just friends?"

She hesitated, then smiled. "Then we'll see how the date goes."

CHAPTER FOURTEEN

Dear Mom,

Airports... Have I mentioned how much I hate them? I managed to stuff all my luggage into a backpack so I could avoid check-in, but still, there's no food. I'm starving and everyone is looking at me like I'm a lunatic because I mentioned stopping at a restaurant before going to get dressed for the thing tonight. Dinner isn't being served until eight and we have to be ready at five for the step and repeat (whatever that is). I'm hungry now! Maybe the hotel has a minibar with candy I can steal. I can always dream.

Your ravenous daughter,
Angela

ANGELA HELD HER BREATH as Amarilla tightened the last strap of the lime green dress in place on her arm. "It's official, I'm a walking advertisement for the carnival."

"I'm wearing bright orange."

"It suits you." Angela twisted a few times. "You can't see any naughty bits, can you?"

Amarilla tilted her head. "In that dress it's all naughty, but there's no nip slip. Relax." She rested her hands on Angela's bare shoulders. "It's just dinner."

"Plus a million people with microphones and cameras."

She tried to tug the bust line up a little. "If I lean forward I'm going to fall out. This dress was not designed with any regard for my personal modesty."

Amarilla grinned and shrugged. "Don't lean forward."

"Ladies." Jacob walked into the room without knocking and spun around in his raspberry-colored suit. "Aren't we a delicious looking confection?" He winked at Amarilla and then gave Angela a once-over. "I would love to see that dress rumpled on the floor."

"So would I, but not next to your suit," Angela muttered. "Where are my shoes?"

Amarilla grimaced, wiggling a foot. "The cute white ones with the low heel?"

Angela glared down at Amarilla's feet. "You stole the only decent shoes. That's mean!"

"Here." Jacob tossed her a pair of silver T-straps with six inch heels.

"Ha." Angela threw them back on the floor. "No. Not only would I tower over everyone in those, but I would fall and break my ankle." She dumped the contents of the studio-provided shoe box onto the bed and picked through the designer torture wear. "Does anyone who designs these things actually wear them?"

Amarilla sat on the edge of the bed and held out a pair of canary yellow shoes with fake feathers. "I don't think so."

"Executive decision time," Angela said. "I'm wearing flip flops."

"You can't wear flip flops on the red carpet!" Amarilla protested.

"My skirt will cover my feet," Angela replied stubbornly. "It's flip flops or barefoot."

Jacob stroked his chin thoughtfully. "Go barefoot. If someone gets a picture they'll say you're quirky. Flip flops will get you in trouble." He clapped his hands. "We've got to go or we're going to be late."

Angela grabbed her purse. "I feel like a zoo exhibit. All we need is a parrot and my day will be complete."

They were ushered down a roped-off sidewalk into a netted pavilion in front of the conference center. Someone had done their best to turn a quarter-acre of urban environment into a flower-strewn meadow, complete with babbling stream. Butterflies flitted under bright lights.

Jacob bumped her shoulder. "Don't stare. Last year they constructed a huge aquarium so that it looked like we were under the sea."

"Lots of mermaid gowns," Amarilla added. "I'd just signed my contract so I wound up in this hideously bright pink sequined thing." She shuddered in mock horror.

Jacob took her hand and squeezed gently. "This is easy. We stop at each station, smile, chitchat with whoever is standing around, and then move to the next. When we get to the door we can go inside and relax."

"Why are we doing this again?" Angela tried to pull herself in, fighting to ignore all the emotions swirling around her. This was a noisy group, a mob fueled by obsessions and hate. Her head started throbbing. She squeezed Jacob's hand tightly. "I don't want to do this."

"You'll be fine. Amarilla and I will protect you from those mean ol' cameras," Jacob said as he put a hot hand on her back.

She pulled away from him as she started to sweat. "I don't feel so good."

Amarilla rearranged the strap covering the scar on her arm. "Fake happy. Big smiles, eyes wide open. Fake it."

Angela allowed herself to be swept along in the stream of starlets being photographed. She smiled as she burned under the lights. When the cycle of photography finally led to the main entrance, she went looking for the director. Patrick and Geoff

Swendon were taking advantage of the open bar on the foyer. "Mr. Swendon?"

Both of them turned to her. Patrick, the director of *Fractured*, smiled. "Did you survive?"

"No, not at all, I feel so sick. Can I go home now?"

"Oh?" Patrick fixed a flyaway hair. "It's just dinner."

Time was ticking and Delilah was probably tapping her toes with impatience. "I have a killer migraine and—" She covered her mouth with her hand and grimaced.

Swendon frowned. "All right, we can cover for this. We'll shuffle people around at our tables a bit so no one notices a gap. You need to be back here by ten forty-five, and no later. Get changed into the gown you're wearing for the party tonight. The studio sent everyone a couple of choices."

Angela bit her tongue on her first response. The studio had sent her a hideous yellow leather corset and mini skirt for the first red carpet. It probably went with the canary shoes. "Yes, sir. I'll be back. I just need to close my eyes for a little bit. All those bright lights..." She trailed off into a shrug.

"Let's get you out of here without a fuss. There must be an activities facilitator somewhere nearby." Swendon pulled her into a back hall and scanned the crowd of tuxedoed waiters, most of whom were wearing their designer clothes better than the talent waiting to be served.

Cutting through the mob like a shark was a woman in a pristine chocolate brown suit and a conservative updo. She approached them with a tight smile. "Can I help you?"

"Miss David needs to go back to the hotel for an hour or so. Health concerns. Hush hush. We'd rather it be a discreet exit and re-entry."

"Naturally," the woman said. "This way, Miss David."

Angela followed after her sister with relief. "I was worried you wouldn't make it in."

"Oh ye of little faith." Delilah eyed her up and down. "Are you shorter than me?"

"I'm barefoot."

Delilah twitched an eyebrow up in condemnation. "Somewhere in our ancestry I'm sure there's a savage who's proud you've kept up the old ways."

"Amarilla stole my shoes!"

Delilah pushed open a back door and motioned to a waiting cab. "In. You can change in the back seat."

"Won't the cabbie notice?"

"Freddie? He might, but he's my minion so it's not like it will matter."

Angela climbed in and peeked at Freddie, who was indeed a warty green minion from her father's lab. "How'd you rate a minion?"

"I asked." Delilah shoved a box at her. "Clothes. Put them on. Including the stockings, please. We'll fix your hair and makeup after."

Angela eyed the new outfit dubiously. "I have to go back to the party."

"One bridge at a time, sister mine. One bridge at a time." Delilah handed her a sheaf of papers. "The judge was taken to a party and there's video. He looks drugged, but either way the scandal would ruin his career and marriage. Oddly enough, I think it's the marriage that he's most worried about losing."

"A nice change." Angela sorted through the paperwork as Delilah fixed her hair. "What's this? The earring stuff?"

"I told you Tyler Running Fox was the one who bought it. I was able to find surveillance footage."

Angela turned on the dome light so she could get a better view. "That's not Ty," she said through gritted teeth.

"Looks like him to me. The computer made a ninety-five percent match."

Angela shook her head. "This is his stunt double."

"And you know this how?" Delilah leaned over to scrutinize. "I thought Running Fox wasn't a person of interest in your love life."

"He's not, but I've worked with him." She put the papers down. "Do you ever just run on a hunch? No evidence. No data. Just... I've got this feeling."

Delilah lifted an eyebrow in distaste. "Not if I can help it."

Angela studied the picture again. "I'll find some evidence then."

"You think Running Fox is a good guy?"

"I don't think he's a criminal." She handed the picture back to Delilah. "That's Mikey, my next door neighbor. He promised his sister that he would clean up his life. There was a new job, something big. It was going to make everything better. Luiz is dirt-poor, she's counting pennies from the couch just to make ends meet. She's saving everything she can to send her daughter to a better school. Mikey promised her she wouldn't have to anymore, and then he was arrested for a DUI.

"The same week the three bandits became the two bandits. I'm willing to bet Mikey was the bagman and the laundry runner. He's Tyler's stunt double. Someone who's only seen Ty in the movies would probably buy it, and someone coming in with that kind of cash, it makes sense." She shrugged. A nice theory, but what did it all mean?

The taxi slowed to a stop in front of a grim detention center. "Freddie, circle the block and check for watchers," Delilah ordered her minion.

"Problems?" Angela asked, shucking out of her lime green pseudo-dress.

"Everything about this screams trap. The Company has done everything in their power to draw you out. Have you checked your social media accounts?"

"I saw. Everyone hates me."

"Did you see the, 'I've known she'd do something like this for years!' comments?" Delilah asked. "You met all those people in September when school started, but their accounts say differently. Someone wanted you to come and defend your good name."

"So why are we going to a detention center instead of meeting the judge somewhere safe?" She shimmied into the pencil skirt Delilah had given her and pulled on the blouse.

Delilah checked herself in the mirror and smiled. "The judge was blackmailed into not giving Travys a trial by jury. Tricky, but sometimes sentencings don't need juries. That didn't keep The Company from presenting evidence. Travys was locked away because the judge believed he was guilty. I promised to make the blackmail disappear if he gave us a fair hearing. Presenting you as alive and well, plus the testimony of Travys, should solve everything. Off the record. On the record is a whole other mess, but I have my team working on the paper trail."

Angela frowned, pausing halfway into the suit coat. "I need minions."

Delilah handed her a makeup compact. "When we get in there, stay calm but talk fast. And don't cling to Travys. The Company made serious accusations about your relationship with him. Act distant."

Angela nodded, pulse hammering. *Hold on, Travys. I'm coming for you.*

CHAPTER FIFTEEN

Dear Dad,

How does Delilah rate a minion chauffeur and all I ever have are spies? I need minions who listen to me. Preferably, some that can blend in with a classroom environment.

Going back to school soon,
Angela

FREDDIE PULLED UP BESIDE the gate.

"Show time," Delilah said as she checked herself in the taxi mirror one last time. "Let me do the talking to start with."

The walk to the side door of the detention center was as dark and foreboding as the red carpet had been bright and forcefully cheerful. Angela followed her sister like an obedient puppy, eager to get in and be done. Travys could have his life back, she could have her life back, and everything would finally be over. She'd give The Company the slip and get back to what she loved.

Delilah held the door for her. "Any weapons I should know about?"

"I never was interested in them."

A night guard looked at their IDs and ran Delilah's purse through a scanner, but he seemed unsurprised by the late hour visit.

The judge waited for them in a small, bare room with cracked linoleum and water stains on the ceiling. "Miss Samson," he said, holding out a hand to Delilah.

Delilah took it and shook perfunctorily. "Judge Bronson, it's a pleasure to see you again. Thank you for accommodating such a late meeting."

The judge made a dismissive gesture. "I'm old. I don't need sleep as much as I need my curiosity assuaged." He studied Angela as he sat down. "Is this the evidence you said you had?"

"Indeed," Delilah said. "This is Angela Smith, the teacher Travys Freeman was found guilty of murdering."

"Hello," Angela said, braving a small smile.

"Where have you been?"

Delilah rested a hand on her shoulder. "She was recovering from the shock at her parents' home in Texas. It wasn't until my firm called her parents about the details of her burial that Miss Smith even knew there was a problem."

The judge gave Angela a critical look. "You don't watch the news?"

"My father has high blood pressure and the politics get him worked up. I tried checking online, but I couldn't find a trial date." The judge made eye contact and Angela had no problem with letting the guilt build.

He coughed. "There were problems with the trial."

"That much is painfully apparent," Delilah said crisply. "Where is Mr. Freeman?"

The judge sighed. "We have him in a holding cell in anticipation of his release. And I'm not saying I'll release him, either. This is... not what I intended. There's the whole question of why Mr. Freeman had the gun in the school in the first place. That's enough for me to keep him in jail."

"Not without trial and the benefits of counsel," Delilah said. "What you've done is illegal. That boy has a right to trial with a jury of his peers. You either provide him with that trial and have it dismissed for contempt of court, or we sort this out tonight in a quiet way that serves justice and preserves your reputation."

Judge Bronson glowered at Delilah.

She raised an immaculately sculpted eyebrow. "You are the one who created the situation, Judge

Bronson. I'm simply providing a way for you to correct your error."

The judge reached for his pen, and stopped. "No. No more mistakes. I need to know why Mr. Freeman had a gun on school property. He won't tell me, but I assume you have an explanation."

"He was going to commit suicide," Angela said. "His father was abusive and Travys didn't want to deal with it anymore. He didn't shoot at me. I tried to get the gun when he shot at himself."

Delilah squeezed her shoulder. "Stop growling," she whispered. "Judge?"

Judge Bronson looked from Angela to Travys. "Do you think sending him back to that situation will help?" He held up a hand. "I understand your concern, Miss Samson. I'm not saying the boy needs to stay here, but I won't countenance sending him back to a dangerous home environment that inspired him to attempt to take his own life once. Unless you have arrangements made, he will stay here until child protective services can be called in to evaluate the situation."

"Happily," Delilah said, reaching into her briefcase, "I foresaw such an argument and took it upon myself to have our firm follow up with his mother and a sponsor." Delilah presented the judge with a small dossier. "The Bright Hope sponsor network has matched Travys with one of their patrons. Travys's mother has signed the necessary paperwork and he has been enrolled in a private school in

Virginia. He'll receive room and board, an excellent education, and the sponsor will cover the cost of his first four years at any university as long as he maintains a three-point-oh grade average or better."

Judge Bronson's brows knit together as he reviewed the paperwork. "Very thorough. Everything here was done in anticipation of his release."

"Either now or as the result of a trial." Delilah shrugged as if to say that minor detail meant nothing to her. "Travys Freeman was imprisoned and found guilty of first degree murder without trial. Standing in front of you is his alleged victim. If Travys doesn't walk out with us tonight our next stop will be a meeting with a *New York Times* journalist. Tomorrow morning, Travys will leave for his new school, or your name will be plastered over every morning talk show in the country."

The judge scowled at Delilah and Angela's throat constricted with fear. "I don't appreciate blackmail, Miss Samson."

"This isn't blackmail," Delilah replied. "You made choices, and you will deal with the consequences like a responsible adult. I won't coddle you because you're in a position of power. You aren't an infant."

The judge was still waffling. Angela focused on agreement, on his desire to do good, and a sense of right, wrapping it all up and nudging it at him.

With a heavy sigh, the judge nodded. "Fine. I'll sign the release paperwork." He looked up at Delilah. "And the rest?"

"The blackmail The Company used will be gone by noon tomorrow. I suggest sticking to public places and avoiding your phone."

Delilah paced while they waited for Travys to be released and change into his street clothes.

"Will you stop doing that?" Angela asked. "Everything's fine now."

Her sister shot her a dark look. "Let's get out of the city before we declare this a roaring success."

"You're making me nervous."

"Good." Delilah checked her watch. "Do you have your phone?"

"Always."

"Check the social networks. Keywords 'superhero' and 'Bugman.'"

Angela pulled her phone out of the little purse she was wearing and typed in the commands. "Is there a reason for this?"

"Some people track superhero sightings." Delilah glowered at the guard.

Angela snuck a glance in his direction, then hit him with the desire to sleep. Everything is fine, she whispered to his mind, relax. Sleep. He sighed, settled back, and didn't even notice when his phone clattered to the floor.

Delilah scooped it up with gloved hands. "Our friend here was texting a buddy, 'Sketchy stuff tonight. Two hotties visiting the judge after hours.'"

"That's not technically illegal. Is it?"

"Depends on who he was sending the message to." Pulling a thin wire from her pocket, Delilah connected the guard's phone to hers. "Let's have a peek at his contacts list."

Angela frowned. "Downloading information from another person's tech without consent is illegal. I paid attention to that part of my Ethics and Law class."

"Super villain!" Delilah said with a cheerful smile. She unplugged the phone as Travys walked around the corner in the same jeans and T-shirt he'd worn when he was arrested. There was a small ketchup stain on the bottom of his shirt, a leftover from lunch.

No, Angela realized with sobering unease, a bloodstain. Her blood. Heaven above, that had been close. It was almost enough to make her believe in miracles.

Travys blinked at her in confusion. "Miss Smith? They said you were dead!"

"A gross exaggeration," Delilah said. "Shall we get going? There's a cab waiting for us."

"We'll get you some fresh clothes on the way." Angela held out a hand.

Travys stepped around her as he headed for the door. "Where's my mom?"

She touched his mind too, felt the unease and despair that hadn't been addressed while he was incarcerated. He was confused. Lost in a sea of his own fears and a danger to everyone.

Angela glanced at Delilah as she bit her lip.

"Your mother is out of town, but we hope she'll be in contact with you soon."

Travys's face shut down, and then he seemed to shrug it off.

"She would have been here if she could," Angela said.

"No she wouldn't. She's always leaving, my mom. Always making plans to get the money so she could go somewhere else." He stopped at the door. "I'm not going back to live with Chris. I ain't doing that."

"You've been enrolled in a very good school in Virginia," Delilah said. She opened the door and nodded for Travys and Angela to follow. "I'll make sure your mother calls as soon as she can."

As they walked out of the detention center, Angela tugged at the curl of confusion until it straightened out. It was the least she could do. Her nerves twanged with the need to put everything right.

Travys stepped out of the detention center and took a deep breath of fresh air. Shoving his hands in his pockets, he looked up at the overcast sky with a smile. "The moon's playing peek-a-boo. I missed that. Is that stupid? I was locked up and I didn't miss TV or my mom. I missed seeing that moon. Like, it's always there when nobody else was."

"That's very poetic," Angela said.

"Poetry later, leaving now," Delilah said. "We all have places to be and—"

A plume of dust shot up in front of them. Under the weak streetlight and the peek-a-boo moon, the person who landed in front of them was recognizable as the superhero Bugman. When he smiled light glinted off his white teeth.

Angela decided to hate him on principle. Real people did not have teeth that shone in the moonlight.

"Going so soon?" the superhero asked as he sauntered forward. "Well, well, well, how cliché. The villainess, her sidekick, and the hag."

"Who are you calling a sidekick?" Delilah demanded.

"Who are you calling a hag?" Angela wished she'd left her hair down so she could toss it around as a physical punctuation to her question. Sometimes life had no sense of narrative.

Bugman pointed at Travys. "Did you really think you'd get away with this?"

Angela pulled her student back. Chin lifted, she glared at him. "Travys did nothing. He was wrongfully incarcerated. If you really represent justice"—Delilah snorted in disbelief—"you will let us walk away unmolested."

The sneer on Bugman's face was nearly as frightening as the leer she'd grown accustomed to seeing on Pyro. "Criminals must be punished. This boy shot you, Miss Smith." He dragged her name out in a mocking way better left to the playground.

"I'm not dead. Habeas corpus, sir. No corpse. No conviction."

"By tomorrow morning, you will be a corpse. And you"—he pointed at Delilah—"will be back in Company headquarters where you belong."

Delilah's eyebrows were lost under her fringe. "Which company?" she asked, feigning confusion. "My company headquarters? Yes, I'm expected there. That's the thing about reality. Those of us who live in the real world are expected to show up at work every day. And not wear spandex." Her lips curled into a grimace of horror. "Halloween is over, and padded codpieces are not in fashion."

Bugman made the mistake of looking down at his crotch.

Delilah had her gun trained on the superhero in the blink of an eye.

"Put it away," Angela ordered with an emotional shove that would have turned most people into voluntary slaves. Decades of sisterhood and a stubborn streak the size of the Rio Grande made Delilah immune. She didn't even acknowledge Angela. "Please," Angela begged. A cold breeze ruffled the loose hairs on her neck. "Please, don't do this."

"Listen to the teacher," Bugman said. "There's no way you can—" He froze midstep, wreathed in blue ice.

Angela leaned forward. "Bugman?"

She felt someone move behind her. "Aren't you

supposed to be on the red carpet tonight?" a soft voice whispered.

CHAPTER SIXTEEN

Dear Travys,

I'm writing this on the flight into New York, and I hope I'll be able to hand it to you in person tonight.

First, I want to apologize for all of this. It was selfish of me to go into hiding like I did. I thought I was protecting... Well, everyone really. Myself, my family, my mom most importantly.

I know that doesn't make much sense, but if you ask me one day I'll tell you the story of the man who tried to destroy my family. He left my mother broken. It took her years to heal, and The Company supported him in what he did.

I promised myself when I was little that I would never let the superheroes bully my family again.

And in doing that I broke the promise I made to all of my students on that first day of school.

I remember how you came in, shy, and skinny, and just a little scruffy. You were hiding in the back row under that torn brown hoodie you loved so much. My heart broke a little because I could see how curious you were. You soaked in the first few lessons but I could never draw you out of your shell.

And then one day you asked a question. That was one of the best days of my life. I felt like I'd accomplished something real. I'd connected with a student and made you interested in math. That's geeky, but for a teacher it's huge.

Travys, you are such a bright, wonderful, intelligent young man. You are going to do great things. The whole world is waiting to open up for you. And I'm going to make sure you get the chance to explore it.

Sincerely,
Miss Smith

ANGELA WHIPPED AROUND AND found herself nose to nose with Arktos.

The safety of Delilah's gun clicked off. "We are behind schedule, ladies and gentlemen. Everyone I like, to the car please. All strangers in spandex get to stay here."

Arktos took Angela's hand before she could move away. "Are you hurt?"

She shook her head.

"We need to go," Delilah insisted, pulling Travys behind her and urging him toward the waiting taxi.

Angela shook her head. "Give me a minute."

Delilah flicked the safety back on. "You'll be late."

"Please? Sixty seconds."

"I promise she'll be quick," Arktos said. "Bugman won't stay frozen forever."

Angela shivered. "Did you kill him?"

"No, I chilled him, it's like stasis. He'll thaw in a few minutes and never know the difference. Except you will be gone."

Delilah put her gun away. "Sixty seconds. The clock is running," she said before hurrying after Travys.

Angela licked her lips and then risked looking into Arktos's eyes. "What are you doing here?"

A gentle smile played about the corners of his mouth. "Rescuing a damsel in distress?"

"I think the lawyer might object to being called a damsel."

He shrugged. "I kept seeing the detention center and knew you were getting into trouble. I thought you might want backup."

"Do you realize how much trouble you're going to get in for this? The Company is not going to see me as the good guy here."

His gaze became intense. "They can consider it my resignation."

Angela jerked back, bumping into the frozen Bugman. "Resignation?"

"I read the file on this case." Arktos raised a shoulder and shrugged it off. "There's no way to put a positive spin on locking a kid up because you want to use them as bait. I've got a little brother. I can't risk someone deciding he's a pawn to be played with.

So I'm out."

Angela shook her head. "You can't quit."

He chuckled. "I still have my day job. You know, the one that pays the bills?"

She shook her head harder. "No, I'm serious. Leaving The Company is suicide. You can't walk away from them."

He twitched an eyebrow. "You haven't had any trouble."

Angela rolled her eyes. "I have plenty of trouble, but I also have my family. We're good at handling tough situations. Who will be there for you?"

"You?" He gave her a look like a lost little puppy.

She blinked.

The quiet night grew loud around them. "Angela?"

Her jaw dropped. "I... Um. We need to talk about that."

"Hardly." He leaned in and dropped a chaste kiss on her lips.

She didn't mean to, but she found herself following him as he pulled away, chasing down another touch.

Arktos drew her close. "You're going to be late for the ball, Cinderella." He stroked the side of her face. "See you on the red carpet tonight?"

"Yes."

He caught her hand before she grabbed his mask. "No cheating." Arktos kissed her palm. "Would you still rather hear your dog bark at a crow than a man swear he loves you? When you depart from me, sorrow abides and happiness takes his leave."

The taxi horn blared behind them. "Sixty seconds is up!" Delilah yelled from the back seat. "Get in the car or walk."

He blinked. "Charming lady."

"Did I mention I come with relatives?" Angela winked, grinning. "I guess—"

Delilah stormed up with a manila folder in her hand. "Take this." Delilah shoved the folders at Arktos as she grabbed Angela's arm. "You," she said to Angela, "are coming with me."

Angela was impressed that she made it to the car without breaking her ankle. "Was it that important to leave right now?" she demanded as she slammed the door behind her. "Really? I wanted to get his name!"

"You don't know it?" Delilah stared at her. "You told him your real name and you don't know his?"

"Um..."

"Angela Shalom Meredith Smith, you are the stupidest thing I've ever seen since Gideon decided to collect a box of rock pets and named them all Herbie." Delilah's eyes slid to Travys in the front passenger seat. "Hell, woman, there's even a witness."

Travys sat up in alarm.

"I've always used my legal name," Angela said. "Travys knew who I was all along. I talked about our family in class. I'm not ashamed of who we are."

"You never mentioned the whole superpowers thing," Travys said.

"What superpowers?" Angela asked. "Do we look like we're wearing spandex?"

"Your boyfriend does," Delilah snipped.

Angela crossed her arms and fell back into the leather seat with a hmph. "He's not my boyfriend."

"No, he's the guy you were kissing whose name you don't know. Mother will be so pleased."

Delilah dodged the shin kick, so Angela contented herself with sticking out her tongue. "I know his name."

"What is it?"

"I don't need to tell you. Not unless we're serious, and we aren't. Arktos... I was telling him good bye." She could feel the pull of Delilah's power, the subtle desire to tell her sister everything. "I won't see him again. Ever."

"Darn right you won't." Delilah pulled out another folder from her briefcase. "This is your new driver's license, state ID for Virginia, and the emails you've been exchanging with Redbrick Academy. Travys's school is hiring a new computer teacher. It's not your area of expertise, but you can fake it. 'Here's a mouse, go click. Here's a keyboard, go type.'" Delilah mimed teaching.

Travys giggled. "I could teach that class."

Angela stared at the papers. "Leave L.A.? Why... No. I can't leave L.A. right now."

"You went there to lay low for a bit. It's not my fault you started a new career!"

"You have a new job?" Travys looked at her in confusion.

"I've been acting." Angela pushed the paperwork back at her sister. "I've got commitments. Contracts. People are expecting to see me."

"What about Travys?" Delilah demanded.

"What about Mia and Aaron?" Angela shot back. "Who's going to tutor them? Who's going to step in on *Fractured*? Travys is going to be fine. He's going to a good school, I can keep in touch with him by email, and by this time next week his mom will be there."

Delilah stared at the roof of the car in her classic Counting To Ten And Praying For Patience pose. "This is about Arktos, isn't it? You're going to risk everything to play tonsil hockey with a superhero."

Angela rolled her eyes. "This has nothing to do with Arktos. I told you, we're through. This is about being a responsible adult and not leaving my coworkers jobless because suddenly there's a little risk associated with living there."

"It's not a little risk!" Deliah shouted. She took a deep breath and let it out with a huff. "Listen," she said in the voice Angela knew as Delilah Being Reasonable While Telling Everyone What To Do, "you can't honestly think going back to L.A. is a good idea. It's not. The facts are black and white. I understand that you want to be responsible, and it's a very noble ideal, but you need to check back in to reality. You are not AJ David, movie star, you are Angela Smith, math teacher."

Delilah reached over and patted her hand. "I'll make some phone calls and by morning roll call this will all be a bad dream. You'll be teaching again on Monday. Isn't that what you really want?"

Angela caught herself nodding and stopped. "Delilah! Stop messing with my head! I'm going to L.A. The end. I'm not arguing with you."

"Only because you know there is no logical argument for your actions."

"I have loose ends I need to tie up." Angela tapped on Freddie's shoulder. "Take me back to the conference center, please."

Delilah slammed back into her seat, arms crossed.

Travys grinned nervously. "I'm so glad I'm an only child."

"Don't think I'm not envious," Angela muttered.

Delilah rolled her eyes as the cab stopped outside the center. "I don't like this plan."

"Objection noted."

"I don't like Arktos."

"I wouldn't let you kiss him anyways."

"That green dress was hideous on you."

"Agreed."

Delilah huffed. "Be careful?"

"As careful as you always are."

Her sister winced. "Try to be a little more careful than that. You don't know how to get handcuffs off."

Arktos thumbed through the files as soon as he landed at the small Company safe house outside the city. No one seemed to remember it existed and he doubted anyone would look for him there. Not when he was supposed to be highly visible on the red carpet in under an hour.

Mikey's photo on the first page came as a gut punch. Glee's was no surprise; he'd wondered about that since her first wig went missing. For the pyro there were two pictures, Jacob Kapsimolis and Tyler Running Fox with a dainty scrawl that read, "Hunch?" A second, slightly neater author had written, "Not Ty." underneath.

He sat down at the ancient computer and logged into The Company's remote access portal. Katrina liked to operate everything on a need-to-know basis, but right now that suited him. He found his file, erased it. Found Angela's, erased it. Found Zephyr Girl's, erased it.

A few little clicks and everything vanished into the ether.

Arktos checked his watch: time to fly. There was a red carpet waiting for him.

Not that the cameras mattered, he thought as he changed. Omnipresent cameras were part of life in L.A. No, this red carpet was special because AJ would be there. The gem-encrusted confection she'd worn earlier had left him speechless. Tonight? He adjusted his tie. Maybe tonight she'd recognize him.

CHAPTER SEVENTEEN

Dear Daddy,

I need you to come out to L.A. and I need you to bring your Agree With Me Ray. There's... I'm compromised. That's the right spy term isn't it? When things go all fluffy shaped and everything is wrong?

There's this guy who needs to forget I exist. I think he's working up to ask me for something I can't give. I don't want to hurt him. I don't know if I could send him away. But he's such a nice guy. He can't live on our side of the tracks. He's in love with me, but he doesn't know the family. He doesn't know about Maria. And I can't let him near Mom.

He's Company.

Please, get here as fast as you can. Maria will bring you if you ask. She'll understand. People that come into our lives are in danger every second we're with them.

Please, Daddy, hurry.
Angela

ANGELA SLIPPED INTO THE sound stage's only bathroom with a working air conditioner, leaving the lights off, and locked the door. Swendon had given everyone a long lunch so he could work out some details of the script, and that suited her just fine.

The phone rang. "Hey, Button."

"Hey, Daddy." Angela slid down the door and sat on the cool tiles in the glow of the emergency lighting. "How are things?"

"Better here than there from the sound of it. Do you want to give me the whole story?" he asked with the same patient tone he'd used on Blessing after she wrecked the car for the third time.

"Not really. It makes me sound like a twitterpated idiot."

"That happens sometimes. I did incredibly moronic things at your age." She heard the sigh of leather as he settled back in his favorite chair. "Who's the guy?"

"Arktos, the main superhero for the region."

"And he's in love with you?"

"It's not my fault! I told him it would never work." Angela wiped a lone tear from her eye. "I didn't mean to break cover. There was just... The people were scared and hurt. I thought I could go in, rescue them, and get away without anyone caring. I don't dress like a superfreak, so you know, maybe I could be just a good citizen."

"Mmmhmmm." Her father's dubious tone came through loud and clear. "Sweetie, I may think you're cute as a button, but the rest of the world hasn't spent a lifetime around you and your sisters and your mom. I don't want to sound harsh, but there is literally no way I can think of aside from radical cosmetic surgery that will let you blend in with everyone else."

She rolled her eyes. "Daddy, I'm in L.A. Every other woman is a hot blonde with long tan legs. I don't have a monopoly on this look, you know."

"Are they all as smart as you?"

She stuck a tongue out at the phone before responding. "No. But no one has asked me my IQ. That would be weird."

"You're still an intelligent, down-to-earth, easy-going, beautiful young woman who is going to turn heads. I tried to talk your mother into letting me enroll you in a Swiss priory with barefoot nuns chanting hymns for this very reason. I thought I made a very rational argument. I even had a Power-Point."

Angela giggled. "Never mind that we aren't Catholic."

Her father sighed. "Do you love this guy?"

"No."

"Really?"

"I haven't even known him a month, Daddy. Love doesn't work like that. It's not eyes-across-a-crowded room and bluebirds singing."

"Fine, so it isn't marriage-and-a-baby love. He's a horrible man troll who is threatening you?"

"I didn't say that." Angela studied at her fingernails. "It's just... We got too serious too fast. I'll take some of the blame. He's easy to like. Smart. Funny. He quotes Shakespeare all the time. You'd like him," she said without thinking.

"So you want to rip his heart out and put it in a blender because...?"

"Daddy!" Angela frowned at the phone, appalled. "I didn't say that. I said I want him to forget about me. He knows too much already and it won't be long before he figures out who Mom is. What then? What are we supposed to do when a Company superhero finds out that Mom is alive? They'll come for her and then I'll have to kill him for real. This is easier. Better."

There were heavy footsteps in the hall outside and someone tried to open the door. Angela braced herself against the sink. "Occupied!"

"Hurry up!" a man on the other side yelled.

She ignored him.

Her father coughed. "Angela? Do you remember when Rolling Shock took your mom from us? Do you remember how you felt when we went to the park and your mom was there and she didn't recognize you?"

"Yes," Angela whispered.

"Do you hate Arktos enough to hurt him like that?"

"I don't want to hurt him. I'm trying to save him!"

"Then let him decide whose side he's on. If he knows the truth about what happened and he backs The Company, we'll take care of it."

Angela's breath caught and she forced the words out in a whisper. "And what if he proposes?"

"Then we'll set an extra plate at the dinner table. It was going to happen eventually; your mother and I knew it would. Five children do not grow up and stay single for eternity. That's not how life works."

"Daddy!"

The person outside hit the door with something hard. "I gotta go, lady!"

Angela turned her back on the stall door. "I'm not ready to get married!"

"Then ask him out for dinner."

She swallowed and took a long, ever-so-slightly-shaky breath. "Love you, Daddy."

"Love you too, Button."

Angela turned off her phone.

"Hurry up!"

Grumbling, she opened the door. "Good grief, do you think it's easy to pee in this suit?" she demanded as she swept past the gaffer. It wasn't until after he slammed the door that she realized she'd have to hold it until the next break. Stupid men. Stupid phone calls. Stupid shooting schedule. Even superheroes needed to pee sometimes.

* * *

"AJ!" Jacob tackled her with a sweaty hug. "How is my most favorite lady?" A drop of his sweat fell onto her neck.

"Good. Off, now." She pushed him away and tried to focus on the script she was reading.

"We're going out for drinks. Wanna come?" Jacob asked as he played with her hair.

Angela batted his hand away. "Can't. I'm dying tonight." Swendon had decided the easiest way to pick who was getting offed in the season finale was to film everyone dying so he could put off the decision until the very last minute.

Jacob sat next to her and gazed adoringly. "Tell Swendon to cut the talk. Everyone knows Pacifica will survive. You're the fan favorite."

"You have to kill your darlings to make art," Angela countered. She hit him with a light wave of disinterest.

He ignored it. "Come on, Peach. I want some quality time with you. I feel like it's been forever since we did something together."

"That's because we've never done anything together," Angela returned, trying to keep the sarcasm from showing too blatantly. Try as she might, she couldn't make Jacob fit into the mold of Arktos. He was too short, not muscular enough, and he was always grabby. It was getting on her nerves. "Tell you what, I'll call when I'm done shooting and meet you at the bar. You aren't planning to go to bed early, are you?"

"Not if you'll keep me up late." He winked lasciviously at her.

"Great. Have fun!" With a chilly smile she hit him with the urge to walk away, a strong urge. That got through.

Jacob pivoted and zeroed in on his next victim. "Mikey! I was hoping you'd be here tonight. Let's go get a beer. I'll drive."

Angela flipped through the script one more time as the crew reset the scene and someone painted her leg with fake blood. Geoff Swendon meandered through everything, checking the lights and sound.

"Is Pacifica ready?"

"I'm ready." She tossed the script on her chair and walked into the light. "Let's kill me and call it a night."

Three hours later, Angela walked through the dark sound stage alone. While she'd showered, the place had shut down. Even the janitors were gone. It was almost ghostly. Appropriate though, she decided. This was her last day on a film stage, and she was the last one leaving. It had been fun in its own way. A learning experience. Today she was a TV star with a fan following and her picture plastered over a dozen magazine covers. Tomorrow she'd be unemployed and sending her application out to various schools.

Maybe she'd join the Peace Corps so she could travel Africa with Blessing. They could do with a nice bonding experience.

Her ringtone echoed as she stepped into the deserted parking lot. "Hello?"

"AJ, it's Luiz, are you home yet?"

"Not yet. I'll be there in a couple of minutes, why?"

Luiz swallowed a sob. "Somebody jumped Mikey. The police just called me. They're taking him to the hospital. I'm going to go meet them, but I'm onsite for the Clayborn movie and I'm worried about Mia. I don't know where they got him. Can you…" She sniffed. "Can you go make sure Mia's okay? Call me as soon as you get home?"

"Of course. Have you tried calling her yet?" Angela jogged for her bike, stuffing her nonessentials in her backpack as she ran.

"A dozen times, but she won't pick up. She's probably already asleep."

"Don't worry about it. I'll call from the house in fifteen minutes. You go take care of Mikey. I'll stay with Mia until you get home. Luiz"—she focused on her friend, somewhere out there in the city of millions—"it's going to be okay." Angela willed Luiz to believe her. "Mikey will be fine. Mia is fine. We'll make this okay."

"Yup. Good. Okay." Luiz's breath sounded ragged.

"I'm going to hang up now so I can drive. I will call you in fifteen minutes. I promise. Mia is fine."

"Okay. Thank you." Luiz hung up as Angela heard sirens in the background.

She pulled her helmet on and turned the key on her bike. Nothing happened. She tried it again. Nothing. Angela pulled her helmet back off. Leaning down, she checked under the bike. Wires were hanging loose. Someone had sabotaged her bike. What kind of punk move was that? Why would anyone mess with her bike?

A shiver of apprehension rolled up her spine.

Yeah, there were a couple people who might hate her. It probably wasn't hard for Glee to guess who Rage was; they'd been mistaken for each other enough times. Even if Glee hadn't put two and three together to get five Angela was likely on her hit list for everything else that had happened in the past month.

A car turned the corner, moving slowly like a shark on the hunt. Angela stood, holding her backpack by the straps so she could use it as a weapon if someone jumped out. The car glided to a stop in front of her and the window rolled down.

"Are you okay?" Tyler asked.

Angela eyed her bike and then the darkly beautiful actor. "I'm good."

"That's not much of a poker face, AJ. What's wrong?"

Angela sighed, muttering about gambler's chances. "My bike won't start. It's fine. I can call someone for a ride."

"Isn't Luiz working tonight? I heard Clayborn's movie has a motorcycle gang."

Well, wasn't he Mister Well-Informed? She shrugged. "Bike gangs are popular right now." She cursed at her phone. Five minutes wasted. Right now Mia could be... Her mind shut down. She didn't want to think what could be wrong with Mia right now if Mikey had been attacked at the house. She realized Tyler had said something. "What?"

"I asked if you wanted a ride." He sounded more worried than amused.

"Yes, please. I've got to get home." She opened the door and hesitated. "I'm telling you now that me getting into this car isn't a sign that I like you, trust you, or want anything to do with you. I'm not trying to seduce you in any way. I'm desperate. I need to get home. I will give you gas money."

"Understood. I am m'lady's taxi cab." He rolled the window up and gripped the wheel with both hands. "I'm so glad I went to college for this. Very good use of my degree."

CHAPTER EIGHTEEN

Dear Mom,

I'm fine. Daddy's worrying over nothing. Don't worry about it.

Love,
Angela

ANGELA SLID INTO THE soft, heated leather seats in a car interior that was chilled to Spokane Cold. "Where are you from?" Angela demanded, rubbing warmth back into her arms.

Tyler chuckled as he turned up the heat on her seat. "North Dakota."

"Which is in the arctic circle, right?"

"Only a couple hundred miles away. You're from the south?"

She settled back in her seat, letting the warmth pull the stress from her muscles. "I spent most of my life in Texas. You can move around, but it's hard to escape."

"Were you a spoiled southern princess or a cowgirl?"

"Yes." Her phone vibrated against her foot and she picked it up. "Yes?"

"Hey, Peach. Where ya at?" Jacob asked. In the background she could hear dance music.

"I'm leaving the studio. Um, about tonight—"

"That's why I was calling. Mikey and I are getting bored waiting for you."

"Mikey?" she asked, wrinkling her brow as Tyler pulled out of the studio compound onto the main street.

Tyler glanced her way, but she shook her head and he stayed silent.

"You know, Luiz's brother?" Jacob asked. "He's sitting here with me and we're both waiting for you. Even though we both know you like me best."

"Um, Jake, lemme call you back. I forgot something inside." Angela hung up in confusion.

"Something wrong?" Tyler asked as they headed for the highway.

"Jacob wants me to meet him and Mikey at the bar, but Luiz is going to meet Mikey at the hospital because he got beat up. I told her I'd go home to sit with Mia until she can come home. Why would Jacob say Mikey is at the bar if he isn't?"

Tyler switched lanes in the heavy weekend traffic. "Maybe the guy stole Mikey's ID and then got beat up. Seat belt on, please."

"Right." She twisted and a bright red car parked beside the gas station caught her eye. The number plate read JACOB-1.

"AJ?"

She buckled herself in. "It's nothing." Red cars were a dime a dozen in L.A. and there had to be hundreds of Jacobs.

The car merged stealthily onto the highway. "Do you want to talk about it?"

Hundreds of Jacobs. Especially after Twilight. "Hmm? No, not really." She shook her head, then sighed. "I'm sorry. That was rude. It's been a long day. I died. It was a surreal experience. And now this. I'm tired, and worried, and things aren't going the way I want. If I start talking I'll start babbling. I'm already babbling. You don't want that."

They were silent as the miles vanished under wheels far quieter than Angela's thoughts until Tyler finally said, "Are you going to give me an address or am I supposed to guess where we're going?"

"Oh! Sorry. Next exit and make a left."

"That's not the high-rent district."

Angela shrugged. "I didn't have a job when I moved in."

"You could afford somewhere safer now," Tyler pointed out. "You have a job."

She glanced at the clock: 12:13. Stop talking, drive faster. "No I don't. My contract expired at midnight. I'm currently unemployed."

Tyler's eyes widened. "You're kidding me. Geoff can't possibly be planning to kill you off! Pacifica is the best character."

Angela shifted in her seat. "Why do people keep saying that? I have no lines. I stand around like the world's most awkward lingerie model."

"But your faces! You're so expressive." When she looked over Ty was smiling, one of his full-blown, panty-dropping, forget-you-have-a-lover smiles that made him oh-so-popular.

She turned away as soon as she realized she was smiling back. "It doesn't matter. Acting was fun for a bit, but it's not what I came to L.A. to do. Next right." She pointed to the street.

Ty turned on the blinker and slowed. "What did you come here for?"

"To teach. The only reason Luiz hired me was because she couldn't afford a tutor out of pocket."

"Because tutoring and acting are very similar skill sets?"

Angela sniffed. "I haven't been acting. Standing around in a white catsuit doesn't take any skill."

"Making it look anything other than ridiculous does."

She narrowed her eyes. "Do you watch *Fractured*?"

"It's allowed. Don't you?"

Angela quirked an eyebrow. "I already know what's going to happen. Why would I watch it? A left here and then stop by the second streetlamp."

"The dark streetlamp?"

"Yes."

Tyler brought the car to a stop beside the curb. "This really is not the best area for you to be living in."

"It's a poor working-class neighborhood; that doesn't mean everyone here is a criminal." She glowered at her bag as she made sure everything was in it. "What do I owe you for gas money?"

"Consider it payment for the cupcake."

"You remember? You didn't even acknowledge me!"

"I was distracted. Sorry."

He managed to look faintly uncomfortable, but Angela hmphed disdainfully and pulled a twenty out of her wallet. She tossed it on the dashboard. "Thank you for the ride."

"Which window is yours?" Ty asked as she got out.

"Why?"

"So I know you got in safe. There are open hallways and... Listen, humor me. Please?"

Angela's lips twitched in a grimace of surrender. "Second window on the left. I'll turn it on when I get in." She tried not to slam the door; it still closed with a satisfying thud. It figured that the one time she wanted a superhero to come to her rescue Arktos was nowhere in sight.

She took the concrete stairs two at a time and ran headlong into Mia.

"AJ!" Mia grabbed her arm and dragged her down toward the street. "We need to go."

Relief washed briefly over Angela as she realized Mia was okay. "Why aren't you asleep?" she asked as she shifted her backpack to the other shoulder.

"Aaron's stuck on the highway. The bike ran out of gas, and I've got to help him. He's trying to push it but it's uphill. I can't call my mom, she'd kill me! But you can take me, right? All we need to do is go on your bike, get Aaron some gas, and take it back so he can get home."

Angela bit her lip as she counted to ten. "Mia, does Aaron have a driver's license? Any driver's license?"

"Um... No?" Mia's eyes went wide. "Come on, AJ! He's got to get home before his brother does or his brother'll kill him! That's brothercide or something."

"Fratricide." Her eyes strayed to the street to where Tyler was still parked. On cue, the window rolled down. "Give me a minute," she muttered to Mia. Putting on her brightest smile and radiating a desire for goodwill and agreement, she strolled up to Ty's car. "Hi."

"Hi." His smile was warm with no hint of mocking. "Did you forget your key?"

"No, I didn't make it as far as my door. There's a little problem. Mia's boyfriend ran out of gas on the highway and he needs a rescue. Do you think you could possibly, pretty please, drive us over there? I promised Luiz I'd take care of Mia until she got home, and I owe Aaron's big brother for giving me a ride to the airport."

Tyler stared down at the steering wheel for a long moment and then shrugged. "Sure. My sleep schedule's shot anyway. Hop on in."

"Thank you." She opened the door and motioned for Mia to get in the back seat.

Mia climbed in, settled down, and then stared. "AJ?" she asked in a stage whisper. "Is that—"

"Al Capone? Yes he is."

Tyler shot her an amused smile. "I always thought of myself more as the Elliot Ness type."

"What, you're untouchable?" Angela asked as she buckled in.

He winked at her. "You can touch me all you want."

Angela gasped in mock horror. "Mister Running Fox, there is a child in the car!"

"I'm fifteen!" Mia protested.

"Fifteen and about to be grounded for life if your mother ever finds out about this little escapade." Angela glared at Mia. "Please tell me that you didn't do anything that will result in a baby in nine months."

"Ohmigosh! AJ! No! Aaron just came over to hang out. We watched a movie."

Angela raised an eyebrow.

Mia blushed, and then tossed her hair nonchalantly. "We might have made out a little. But that was it! I swear! We kept our clothes on the whole time."

Tyler made a noncommittal noise. "I can think of a couple of loopholes that would—"

Angela hit his shoulder. "Don't give the teenager ideas."

He hit back with a smoldering gaze. "Can I give you ideas?"

Angela gave him a steely glare. "Not this late at night and not when I'm this tense."

His face melted into concern. "Do you want me to turn the heater on the seat up again?"

She snuggled back into the leather. "Yes, please. Mia, what exit is Aaron at?"

"He said he can see the gas station with the green sign."

"Two miles," Angela translated. She leaned her head back and texted Luiz to let her know Mia was all right. The whole boyfriend on a stolen motorcycle bit could wait for morning.

The car accelerated with barely a sound. "There's water in the glove box," Tyler said quietly.

She popped it open without a second thought. "Thank you."

"Are you okay, AJ?" Mia asked, leaning forward.

"It was a long day. No big. I'm good. How'd your math test go?"

"I didn't get a hundred, but only because I didn't show all the steps on the last problem. Mr. Marshall doesn't like it when you combine steps." She gasped. "There he is! On the right!"

Angela swatted Mia's arm down.

Tyler flipped on the four-way flashers as he pulled over.

Angela waited for the car to stop before she hopped out, but only because Mia was in the car and she wanted to set a good example. This would be so much easier to handle with her sisters around. Or Arktos. Someone with super strength who could fly? That would be nice right now. "Aaron! What are you doing?" She heard the car door shut behind her as Aaron toed the ground. "Well?"

"I wanted to see Mia. It's no big deal. All I did was run out of gas."

"You stole your brother's bike! Aaron, what is he going to do when he gets home tonight and you aren't there? The poor man is going to have a heart attack! I can't believe you would do this to him."

"I know how to ride!" Aaron protested.

"That doesn't mean anyone in L.A. knows how to drive! It's Friday night. All it would take is one careless drunk and you're splattered all over the highway. What do you think that would do to your brother? He'd be devastated. Get in the car."

"I'll take the bike down to the station," Tyler said as he walked up beside her.

Her cheeks flushed as she realized she'd just ordered Aaron to get into a car that wasn't hers. "I've got it. I'll get the kids out and we can walk."

"Why don't you take the kids home in the car so no crazy drunks try to play hit the pedestrians? I do know how to ride a bike. Promise." He slipped his hands under hers, taking the bike away.

"I don't think it's a good idea."

"Can you drive a car?"

She stared at him in disbelief. "*Yes!*"

"Then why can't you take mine?"

"I don't want to make you do any more. This isn't your problem."

One eyebrow shot up. "Which of those kids is yours?"

She glanced over her shoulder to the car where Mia and Aaron were whispering ferociously. "Both of them."

"Really?"

"I tutor them." Angela lifted her chin and waited for him to argue her claim.

Tyler just shook his head. "You kill me. Here." He tossed the car keys at her. "I'll be back before you know it."

Angela held the cold keys, and then gave in. "Thank you. I'm sure you had better plans for the evening."

"My grandma raised me to be a gentleman."

"That was sweet of her."

He smiled, and she had to stop herself from leaning forward and kissing him. It was probably his cologne. Wasn't there some expensive man perfume that made women lose their minds? She was pretty certain she'd seen an ad for it at the back of a GQ magazine. That had to be it. With another quick smile she retreated to the car.

"Do not ruin these seats or I will kill you," Angela warned the kids. She adjusted the seat and turned on the heater before pulling back into traffic. "Why does he have the air conditioning blasting?"

"Because it's hot outside?" Aaron guessed.

"I can practically see my breath in here!" She took the off-ramp, and then did a U-turn to go home. The car moved like a dream. As they neared their exit she was beginning to fantasize about long road trips with this vehicle. "Do you think we could make it to the border before Ty noticed his car was missing?"

"He probably has GPS tracking," Mia said.

"That's a darn shame." Angela turned for home. "If I ever become filthy rich I'm buying one. I love this car."

"There's only five in the world," Aaron said.

Angela patted the car fondly. "And I'm sure this one loves me. Maybe Ty will let me adopt it."

"Probably not," Aaron said.

She gave the warm leather seats one last rub. "I know. Come on. Everybody out. We'll wait for Ty to get back and then I'll drive Aaron home." Before the temptation to run off with the lovely car became too much to bear, she put the keys on the dashboard along with another twenty from her purse. "I hope that covers the gas for tonight. I'm broke."

Mia smiled weakly at her. "I'll pay you back."

"Don't worry about it. If my bike was working, none of this would have happened. Well, Aaron being stranded on the highway might have happened, but not the whole hitchhiking with strange men thing. I don't recommend doing this ever again."

A motorcycle turned the corner with a roar, picked up speed, and accelerated before the rider popped a wheelie and slowed.

Angela gasped. "Tyler! Get down—that's not your bike to break!"

He laughed. "But it was fun."

She snatched the bike key from him. "Fun isn't the same as safe."

He leaned closer. "Lots of things aren't the same as safe."

"Your keys are on the dash," she said primly. Angela turned back to Mia and Aaron, who were sitting on the steps. "Okay."

The logistical problem of staying with Mia while taking Aaron home presented itself. Calling her mom or Maria to come babysit seemed like the best idea. Maria would be here in a flash of light if she wasn't occupied. What time was it in Brazil?

"I could stay here," Aaron offered. He sat up. "That's good idea. Right? I'll stay here until morning when Mia's mom gets back from work. She won't mind. I'll sleep on the couch."

Angela frowned at him. "What about your brother? You've already snuck out of the house without permission, stolen his bike, and spent the night unsupervised with your girlfriend. For that matter, what will Luiz say? Mia is going to wind up in a convent under a vow of silence for this. Luiz is going to have a herd of cattle. A whole herd." She glared at both of them, young, stupid, and in love, when she heard someone laughing. "Are you still here?" she asked Tyler. "Don't you have a club to go dancing at or something?"

"Oh, no, this is much more entertaining. I'm excessively diverted." He grinned at her over the top of his car.

"I'm glad someone is happy with this mess." She turned back to the kids. "Mia, you go upstairs. Lock yourself in the house and in your bedroom and stay there until I get back. I can't believe I'm doing this at one in the morning."

"AJ, I'll take Aaron home."

"What?" She stared at Tyler in confusion. "I can't just let you... No. I'll take care of it. We've intruded on your time enough already. It's bad enough that he ran off. I can't send him home with someone his brother doesn't know."

"Angela?" Her name floated in the night air. "I'm his brother."

"Oh," Aaron groaned behind her. "I'm so dead."

Angela stared wide-eyed at Tyler. "That's one of those little details that should have come up an hour ago."

"I'm not supposed to talk about it," Aaron protested. "So I don't have weird people with cameras following me."

Ty shrugged. "You were doing such a good job of chewing him out I didn't want to intrude. Keep the bike for me? You can leave it at the studio lot tomorrow when you go to get yours fixed."

"Are you sure?"

"I wouldn't have offered if I wasn't. Aaron, get in. Angela, I'll wait until your light comes on. Thank you for helping tonight. I would have panicked if I'd gotten home and he wasn't there."

Aaron slunk to the car. Angela grabbed Mia's arm and all but pulled the girl upstairs after her. She flipped on the light, locked the door behind them, and watched as Tyler Running Fox drove away with his little brother.

"Am I really dating..." Mia started, but a look from Angela quelled her.

"Bedtime. Right now. And maybe I won't tell your mom everything. Maybe." Angela waited until Mia was out of the room before she dialed Jacob's number.

"Hiya, Peach. Ready to party?"

"I dunno, why don't you and Mikey come over to my place instead? I don't feel like the club scene tonight." She held her breath waiting for a reply.

Jacob took his time. "Mikey says he doesn't know where you live."

Liar. "Okay, then I'll meet you somewhere. How about the old warehouse we filmed on Monday? Some punk messed with my bike and that's close enough."

"Want me to pick you up?"

"Nah. You can park there and we can walk to the bars." Too many cameras in the studio lot, although she'd bet her entire paycheck that they'd not seen a thing when the wires were cut. "I need some fresh air. See ya soon!"

Mia peeked around the corner. "What are you doing?"

"Go to bed. I need plausible deniability. As far as you know, I was here with you the entire night."

CHAPTER NINETEEN

Dear Maria,

If I become a fugitive in the States will you let me move in with you? This is not entirely a rhetorical question.

Call me,
Angela

TY TOSSED HIS WALLET on the table. "So, you stole my bike and rode across town on the freeway on a Friday night."

"AJ already gave me the lecture," Aaron grumbled.

"But she's not your big brother and I am. I get to yell a little. Don't I?" He ruffled Aaron's hair. "Can't we skip the stupid teenage stunts?"

Aaron crossed his arms. "You go do stupid stuff. What happens when you get killed? I'm supposed to move back in with Grandma? Maybe go to a foster home? That's going to end well." His jaw stiffened.

"I'm not going to get killed."

"You don't know that. Every time you go out you might not come back and it doesn't matter!" Aaron yelled. "You care more about people you've never even met than making sure I'm here. I go out all the time. You've never noticed."

Ty's fists clenched. "All the time?"

Aaron took a step back. "A couple times."

"Fine." Ty took a deep breath. "You're right. I quit."

"No!" Aaron's mouth dropped open. "Don't send me back. I'll be good. Please. I promise, no more stupid stuff."

"I mean I quit superheroing. Last week I turned in my resignation. Katrina thinks it's because I took a rib to my lungs. I told her I can't breathe when I fly. I'm officially not with The Company anymore."

Aaron's eyes went wide.

"I don't have any movies lined up for the summer, so I thought we'd go on a road trip or something. Go see some national parks or something. Get out of the city."

"We could go to Texas," Aaron said.

"I guess. Why Texas?"

"'Cause AJ said she was thinking of moving back home over the summer if she can't get a job here, and I figured since you two were dating we might go see her." Aaron's face lit up with a grin. "She has a pool. I saw pictures."

"Why was she showing you pictures of a pool?"

"It was for a word problem; we had to figure out how many gallons of water we would need to fill the pool."

Ty chuckled. "Yeah, I don't think we'll have an invite to visit her. AJ and I aren't dating." He hung his car keys up on the hook and headed for the fridge.

"But, you drove her home," Aaron said, padding after him. "You let her drive your car."

"Because it was an emergency and because I trust her not to do anything to the car."

"She almost stole it."

"What?"

"She said she was going to adopt the car."

He pulled a gallon of milk from the fridge. "I think this is the first time a woman has been more in love with my car than me." Unscrewing the lid, he took a swig of milk. "I feel really inadequate."

"She likes the heater," Aaron reported. "Maybe you could offer to buy her a blanket and take her for a drive."

Of all the things he could think of doing with AJ and blankets, driving wasn't at the top of the list. "Don't get your hopes up. AJ made it clear she's not interested in me." He opened the fridge again, searching for dinner. "We need to go grocery—"

A vision replaced the contents of his fridge. AJ falling. The pyro holding AJ and dropping her. His hand clenched around the handle of the fridge so hard the plastic cracked.

"Tyler?" Aaron put a hand on his shoulder. "What do you see?"

Ty shook his head. "Nothing. It's nothing." He could see how to save her, where he needed to be... But Aaron needed him more. He'd call the police in the morning. If the pyro was arrested there wouldn't be a chance for AJ to die. It wasn't like AJ was going to go out again tonight. "What are we eating?"

* * *

Angela kicked a rock that skidded across the broken pavement and ricocheted off the brick wall of the warehouse. It was past two in the morning. Logically she knew she should go to sleep and then call the police in the morning. That would be the sensible thing to do. At the moment sensible and her weren't good friends. This needed to end.

Light from a car scraped across the rough brick-work before it fell on her, casting a long shadow. She didn't turn around as doors opened and two slammed shut. "Hey."

"Hey," Jacob said. "Why are we meeting here?" The lights turned off as he locked the car door with an audible click.

Angela turned. "Hey, Glee." The actress was wearing a teeny tiny skirt and a neon green shirt that complemented her neon pink hair. She also had a baseball bat, which brought a new level of fun to the evening's proceedings. Finally, everything felt right. "Cute toy."

"My little friend here?" Glee stroked the wood. "This is just a reminder that bad things happen when you play rough. Friendly insurance."

"Every girl should have a friend," Angela said as she sent mellow vibes out. Jacob slowed, his footsteps dragging a little as he swayed under her power.

Glee kept coming with a smile. "You're a naughty girl, AJ." She tapped Jacob's shoulder with the bat. "She's trying to influence you."

Jacob shook his head and frowned. "What? AJ? Why would you do that?"

"Why would you lie about Mikey being with you?"

"Mikey was getting ahead of himself," Glee answered. "We helped him understand his place in the food chain. Now it's your turn."

Angela flexed her hands, feeling the weight of the fingerless boxing gloves. There were still a few ways to end the evening quietly, but Glee was the epicenter of rage—full of hate and anger—nothing Angela was tossing at her was getting through.

"I used to be a scout for The Company," Glee said. "Their little one-trick wonder, kept on a leash and only allowed out for special occasions, until I met Jacob. With my ability to sense when a superhero is near and his abilities to do everything else, we figured we'd knock this town over. It was going so well until you poked your nose where it didn't belong." There was more between Glee and Jacob than simple friendship; Angela could almost see the emotional connection stretching between the two. Glee was holding Jacob back, keeping him from listening to Angela's empathic suggestions.

She began untangling the psychic knot as Jacob circled around behind her.

"I didn't ask for much, just a chance."

Glee shrugged. "But you decided to help Arktos. Between us, that was a bad choice." Her girlish giggle was out of place.

Angela shuffled backwards, trying to keep both of them in sight. "So what? I'm supposed to apologize and let you beat me senseless?" The emotional thread between her two assailants weakened.

Glee looked shocked. "What do you think of us? We're not thugs, AJ, we're entrepreneurs. Think of us as your local supernatural mafia. There are always entry-level positions."

"I'm strictly freelance, sorry." With one last burst of thought she snapped the line between them.

Jacob moved with blistering speed, a blur of hot red. He brushed against her arm. "Option two: come with me."

Glee groaned in pain. "What did you do?"

"I cut him loose." Angela grabbed Jacob's arm, trying to control his attention. "Jacob, you don't need to do this. I can help you. I can get you a new life away from The Company."

The arm under her hand burned like a stovetop.

"What did you do?" Glee screamed. "He's not stable." She rushed Jacob, clutching at his other arm. "Jacob. Jacob? Come back to me. You need me. You love me."

Angela could feel conflicting emotions of need and hate but none of them belonged to her. Jacob's arm grew too hot to touch and she let go. "What did you do to him?"

"I kept him calm!" Glee snapped. "He needs me! Jacob! Jacob, you need me." She clung to him, hugging him close.

Red and blue police lights lit up the alley. Jacob pushed Glee aside as he turned. "What's that?"

"The police," Angela said scathingly. "You thought I was going to meet Jacob alone?"

"I thought you'd be smart and bring Arktos." Anger and fear poured off Glee in a choking fog.

Flames wreathed Jacob as a car door slammed in the darkness. "Tell them to back down."

"Turn yourselves in," Angela ordered, using all her persuasive abilities to force them both to back down.

Jacob screamed and fire engulfed them.

Luck alone got her shield up in time. Angela and Glee both slammed into the wall. Only a bubble of magnetized air kept them from burning. "Jacob! Jacob, stop! You're hurting Glee!" Angela choked on the fiery air.

Jacob stepped through the fire. He held out a hand. "Come with me. Now. Or she dies."

Angela stood on shaking legs, her attention split between an unconscious Glee and the raging villain in front of her. "Do you promise to let her live?" Behind her back she turned on her phone's GPS. If nothing else Gideon and Dad would be able to track her. "You need to turn down the heat, or I won't be able to come."

Jacob swayed a little, but he nodded. The fires in the alley died, although he kept the police at bay with a wall of flame. "We're leaving."

"What about Glee?"

"She's not the one I want."

Angela nodded. "Let me make her comfortable at least. I... Please?"

"Hurry."

Kneeling, she stripped off her riding jacket and pillowed it under Glee's head. With a sharp tug she ripped her necklace off and left it in Glee's hand. Even if the fire moved toward her the shield would keep her safe. As safe as Angela could make anyone.

"Stop wasting time."

They were airborne before Angela could respond. All of L.A. spread beneath her feet. It would have been beautiful if fear wasn't overwhelming her.

Jacob's hand was hot on her wrist. Where he touched her, the skin burned.

She tried to scream, but the wind swallowed her words. In terror she hit back with the only weapon she had left. Blocking out the pain she focused on calm. On the midnight blue clouds swirling around them. On the ocean on the horizon. On happiness... And Arktos. Tyler's smile as he quoted Shakespeare. The way he was always making her laugh.

"Stop it." Jacob shook her, wrenching her shoulder from its socket. "That's not me. That's not how I feel!"

Angela slipped around his sweaty palm so she dangled by her fingertips. "Jacob!" The words fell behind them as he flew higher. She clutched his wrist with her other hand, heart racing in terror. Out of instinct she tried to connect with the necklace only to remember she'd left it with Glee.

The bitter cold of high atmosphere bit her fingers. She tried to squeeze his hand tighter, hold on somehow so she could survive the madness, but as the freezing air engulfed Angela, she trembled. Millimeter by millimeter she slid out of Jacob's grasp.

Tears stung her cheeks as she tumbled into a freefall high above the Pacific surf. The wind skirled past her ears. She shut her eyes, praying she wouldn't feel a thing past the moment of blistering pain as her body broke.

And then she was sitting comfortably in the air. The city, which had been zooming towards her, hovered below without even a breeze to indicate that she was doing anything more than dreaming. Angela twisted and saw Tyler behind her.

"I thought you were staying home tonight, Lois."

She wrapped her arms around his neck. "Get me on the ground. Please." She didn't open her eyes until she felt her boots sink into wet sand. Heart racing, she stepped back shaking more from fear than the cold ocean spray misting her as the tide came in.

"AJ?" Tyler started to step forward but stopped as she shook her head. "What happened?"

The lights of Palos Verdes twinkled in the distance. "I don't know. I thought... I needed to talk to Jacob." She rubbed the cold from her arm. "I..."

A bright light dawned on the false horizon rushing towards them. Jacob landed a few feet away on the beach, fusing the sand where he stood. A miasma of emotions poured off him.

Angela choked, drowning in the waves of bitter hate rolling off him like heat from a flame.

"Arktos, why can't I get rid of you?" Jacob asked as he stepped forward, leaving a fiery silhouette of a man behind him. Black blisters covered his arms and face; he sank as he walked, the sand beneath his feet turning molten. "I came to Hollywood to be a star and do you know what happened at my very first audition? I went in for the part of Keith Little in the new Code Talker movie. I had the looks, the dark hair, the right skin, I even studied a bit of Navajo for the part. It was Oscar bait the whole way and what happened?" The fires behind Jacob flared with temper.

Tyler's hand closed around Angela's wrist, gently tugging her back. "What happened?" Tyler asked, voice even.

"I lost the part!"

A shield of ice bloomed in front of her as the flames roared heavenward.

"You stole my role!" Jacob raged. "You took away my chance at being a serious actor! All because you were born lucky. I didn't lose the part because you were a better actor but because you were born to the right people." Jacob spat. The wall of ice steamed.

"Born on a reservation into abject poverty isn't the usual definition of lucky." Ty tugged at her arm again. "AJ," he whispered, "I can't hold him back. We need to leave."

"He's hurting." The mental anguish emanating from Jacob was burning through her mental barriers faster than it melted the thick wall of ice. Travys's pain had hurt when she'd tried to absorb some of it, but this—she staggered sideways under the assault. "Please, Jacob." She leaned against the ice. "Let me help you. You hurt. It can be better."

"No. It. Can't." He ground the words out through clenched teeth as his legs burned in the molten sand.

"You can heal. You're a superhero." She clutched at his pain, drawing it in deeper. It was like swallowing a burning knife. The self-hatred dimmed the city lights, made the fire so inviting. If she just stepped into the flames, let them consume her, all the fear and jealousy would burn to ash.

"He took everything I wanted. He stole my life."

The ice wall floated away into the atmosphere. Angela fell forward, head resting in the lava-like sand that bubbled and glowed.

Another capsule of ice appeared and the lava blackened as it cracked. "AJ. Angela. Please, we need to go."

The pain ebbed, leaving her shaking. It wasn't so bad, balanced across two people. She gasped, watched her breath turn to fog in the cold. "He's going to kill himself. He can't even... He doesn't understand he's physically hurt." Angela pushed herself to her feet. "How can I save him?"

"You can't." Tyler's sharp pronouncement made her turn.

"I have to."

"You can't save everyone. It's not possible."

She swallowed the bile rising in her throat. "I have to. I can. He just hurts. I can, can take that away. Make him happy again."

"At what cost?"

Jacob slammed a fist into the ice shield, creating a waterfall.

"Look at yourself," Tyler said. "You're burnt. You're bleeding."

She followed his gaze down to her ripped jeans. Her shoes had burned away at some point and her feet were red, blistering from the heat. There was a hand-shaped burn on her arm where Jacob had grabbed her. "I can save him."

Jacob reached through a hole in the ice and she screamed as her arm burned. Tyler grabbed her, trying to pull her away, but it was too late. She was caught in a maelstrom of emotion. Fear tore through her. Deep despair like she'd never felt before. All of Jacob's emotions, his self-doubts, and bitter self-hatred tore into her.

Tyler held her close. "Let go."

Her knees trembled then buckled.

"Angela, you can only save one life. Choose yours. Please," he whispered. "Stay with me."

She pulled her mind free of Jacob's thoughts and collapsed.

Jacob screamed, his voice rising in a deadly crescendo.

Ice covered her. And then there was darkness.

CHAPTER TWENTY

Aaron,

I'm going to be home late. Don't watch the news.

T

TYLER LEANED AGAINST THE hospital glass watching the surgeon try to perform a miracle as Jacob flatlined for a third time. The doctor in charge shook her head. "Time of death, four-oh-three ay-em."

He turned away in misery. Angela was in a room two floors down, lying in the dark alone. He'd been able to keep Jacob from burning her to death, and he'd flown them both to the hospital as soon as Jacob passed out, but it wasn't enough.

Jacob was dead and it looked like Angela was going to follow.

She lay unresponsive under a white blanket. Monitors were hooked up to her arm but that was it. The triage nurse couldn't find a reason. Psychic burnout wasn't a condition the doctors were willing to acknowledge, but he'd seen it before. When he was training there had been others like Jacob. Like Angela. People who couldn't control the mutations they were born with. People who died pushing their bodies past the limits. Humans weren't meant to fly, or burn, or freeze.

He rubbed a hand against his thigh where he'd seared himself to the bone experimenting with his own powers. The scar had long since healed, but the memory of the pain remained.

There was a soft knock on the door lintel. "Mind if I come in?" The light from the hall illuminated the face of a man in a lab coat. "I'm Dr. Smith. How's our patient doing?"

Ty looked over at Angela's pale face. "Same as she was, I guess."

"What happened?" the doctor asked as he puttered around the bed, checking the pulse on Angela's wrist, and tucking the blanket higher.

"You wouldn't understand."

Dr. Smith smiled. "Try me."

"She's... She's a superhero. She can feel other people's emotions, and she tried to take Jacob's. He's the pyro. Superheroes, superhumans maybe. They're different." Ty took a deep breath and shook his head. "She thought she could save him. I think she was trying to take his emotions away so he wouldn't lose control. It doesn't work like that." He crossed his arms. "We don't work like that."

"Well," the doctor said, "she's in good hands now. Rest and fluids are the best cure for exertion. Now, ah, what did you say your name was?"

"Ty. Tyler Running Fox."

The doctor nodded with a knowing smirk. "The one who played Hamlet? My daughter hated you in that."

"Yeah? You'd be amazed how often I hear that." A lump formed in his throat. He worked his jaw, chewing down the fear. "Will she be okay?"

"She shouldn't even be alive." Dr. Smith sighed, rocking back on his heels. "I don't suppose you had a chance to check the news, but it's bad. The island's on fire. One of the helicopter pilots dropping water brought back footage of the beach; it's glass and ceramic now. If it hadn't been for you, this young lady would be a pile of ash."

Guilt weighed him down. "I didn't save Jacob."

Dr. Smith sighed again. "That's one of those things you learn in this business; you can't save everyone. You'll kill yourself if you try. Come on," the doctor said, taking Ty by the shoulder. "I'll buy you a coffee. By tomorrow morning this will all seem like a bad dream."

They stepped into the brightly lit hall and a shoe came flying from behind them, smacking the doctor in the head and bouncing to the floor. "Daddy!" Angela's outraged cry.

Dr. Smith rubbed his head as he stepped back into Angela's room and flicked on the lights. "Hello, sweetheart."

"Daddy, what do you think you are doing?" Angela sat up in the bed and crossed her arms in a pose that reminded him of Aaron throwing a tantrum.

"I thought this is what you wanted!" the doctor protested.

"I changed my mind."

The doctor made a show of sighing. "Is this what you really want?" he asked Tyler. "For the next eighty years? She's never going to grow out of it, trust me on that."

Angela watched him with wide eyes.

Tyler turned back to the doctor. Now that he knew what he was looking for, it was obvious. Father and daughter shared a nose. "Is Zephyr Girl out in the hall?"

The doctor's dark eyes narrowed. "Zephyr Girl? Why would you ask about her?"

"You are Doctor Charm, aren't you?" Ty circled around the doctor so he could be near AJ. "Angela said her father was a villain."

"And from that you leapt to the conclusion her mother was Zephyr Girl?" The doctor sounded incredulous.

"I concluded that after seeing her once. Pictures of Zephyr Girl are not hard to come by. And it makes sense. You both disappeared at the same time."

"I'm certain Zephyr Girl was reported as dead."

Tyler shrugged. "It makes sense, doesn't it? Two people from opposite sides meet, they fall in love, fake their own deaths, and run off together. It's like Romeo and Juliet with better communication."

Dr. Smith steepled his fingers. "That's an interesting theory. Why don't I buy you a cup of coffee? We can talk about your conspiracy theories and your long day and by tomorrow this whole tragic tale will be no more than a bad dream."

"Daddy!" Angela scowled. "I have another shoe."

The doctor rolled his eyes. "He's really too smart for his own good, darling. It will be much easier for all of us if he just... forgot."

Angela huffed. "You aren't allowed to play mind games with my boyfriend!"

"Boyfriend?" Tyler blinked.

"Or whatever."

"Fiancé?" he suggested.

"How long have you known him?" Doctor Charm demanded.

At the same time, Angela gasped. "Tyler Running Fox!"

"It doesn't hurt to ask!"

Angela slapped his arm.

"I lied. It hurts to ask." He caught her hand and kissed it. Her fingers entwined with his.

Doctor Charm cleared his throat. "I hate to interrupt this charming scene, but if you're awake, my dear, we should get going. Bribes and persuasion can only hold off the curious onlookers for so long, and neither of you are low profile individuals."

Angela winced. "Sorry. I just wanted to talk some sense into Jacob."

"Um..." Tyler squeezed her hand, not sure where to start in breaking the news to her.

"I know he's dead. One of the nurses here must have some latent talents because I can practically read her thoughts." Her face grew pale. "She was a big fan of *Fractured*." A tear slipped out of her eye. "Daddy, what are we going to do?"

"Don't worry. I have a plan."

The blonde woman who walked into the room and shut the door couldn't be anyone other than Zephyr Girl. Her face was Angela's softened by age and graced with fine lines around the mouth and eyes. A few wisps of white streaked her already pale hair. "Dearest, there's a woman named Luiz on the phone demanding to talk to Angela."

"She's my neighbor," Angela said. "I was supposed to be babysitting her daughter tonight."

Tyler held out his hand for the phone. Zephyr Girl handed it over and he put it to his ear. "Luiz?"

"Running Fox? Tyler Running Fox." There was a beep. "I swear I called AJ."

"Yeah, um, she's in the hospital right now."

"*What*?" The scream hurt his ear.

"Minor accident. No big deal. She's checking out soon."

"Why are you with her?" Luiz demanded.

He turned to Angela for support. "Because? Why not?"

Luiz muttered something in Spanish then sighed. "Mickey woke up, wanted to talk to the police. He said Glee jumped him with a baseball bat. He thought someone was with her but he wasn't sure who."

"What did the police say?" Tyler asked.

"They already had Glee in custody. The officer said something about a DUI. I'm not sure. Is AJ really okay?"

"Yeah!" He held the phone out to Angela. "Tell her you're okay."

Angela tucked her hair behind her ear. "Hey, Luiz. I'm good." There was a brief pause. "Oh, no, just a really bad migraine. I felt like I was going to black out so Ty took me to the ER. No big." Another pause. "My bike broke, he drove me home. It's nothing. Uh huh. I'll see you tomorrow."

"Nothing?" Tyler asked.

Doctor Charm started whistling. "This is going to be fun," he said to the beautiful woman snuggling with him in the doorway. "Do you remember our first fight?"

"Mmmhmm, I broke your arm."

"And then I bought you a necklace."

"You bought a computer chip being smuggled in a necklace, took the data, and left me with the hot gems."

"That's what I said."

Zephyr Girl patted him on the arm. "You're adorable."

Tyler pointed a finger at Angela. "That's where you get it!"

"Get what?" She looked taken aback.

"You told me I was adorable on our first date."

She rolled her eyes. "That wasn't a date."

"We went out in public and did things together."

"We stopped a heist together! That's not the same thing as having dinner together." She laughed and shook her head. "It wasn't a date."

He frowned. "I'll cook you dinner. Or breakfast, since the sun is going to be up in an hour."

"Today?"

He smiled at her parents. "I'll cook for all of us."

CHAPTER TWENTY-ONE

Dear Mom,

Next time I tell you I'm fine I'd prefer if you just called instead of unleashing Daddy on Los Angeles. I think that might have been an overreaction. Don't you think?

I mean, yes, convincing the entire city that the whole setup was a stunt for Fractured *and that nothing was really real was great. But I'm not sure letting Daddy use his giant Agree-With-Me-Ray on a city is wise. I think it's going to cause trouble in the future.*

Ty says, "Thank you!" for taking Aaron this week. With school starting on Monday and filming for the movie starting Thursday I didn't think we were going to find time for a honeymoon.

Love and kisses,
Angela

THE HOUSE STILL SMELLED new. Even after moving Aaron's things into his new room and finding he'd packed his gym clothes without washing them first, the house smelled like fresh paint. Ty lit a candle and looked around.

Home.

He'd never really had one growing up. There had been a string of his mom's boyfriends' houses, and then his grandmother's double-wide trailer, but there was never something he wanted to go back to. And now he had a home, and a wife, and in-laws... who were a little bit more daunting than he'd anticipated. Still...

Out by the pool he saw movement. Light from the full moon glinted off Angela's diamond ring as she walked past the pool. He licked his lips, tried to remember how to breathe.

How was it possible for a woman to grow more beautiful every day? The first time he'd woken up beside her with sunlight streaming in so she glowed like the princess from a fairytale he thought he was still dreaming.

* * *

"Hey." Ty kissed her cheek as he walked past to dive into the pool. He surfaced on the far side, treading water and smiling his panty-dropping smile. "Are you going to come swimming?"

Angela dipped a toe in the water to make sure he hadn't chilled it to an unagreeable temperature.

"It's safe," he promised.

"With you in it? I don't think so."

He swam toward her. "What's the worst that could happen?"

"I might lose my bikini again," she said as she sat on the edge of the pool, letting her legs dangle in the warm water to tempt him.

"Mmmm, I don't see that as a problem." He started massaging her calves. "I don't think you mind either." He moved up her legs and then lifted her into the water.

She wrapped her legs around him, bare legs rubbing against bare skin. "What happened to your No Skinny Dipping rule for the pool?"

"We're alone." He kissed her, tongue teasing her lips apart as his fingers nimbly untied her bikini bottom.

She kissed his neck, working her way up to the sensitive spot that made him shiver. "Dost thou love me?"

"Troth, no, no more than reason."

Angela pushed away, gliding through the warm water. "Why then, the world is deceived, for they have said you are much in love with me."

"Peace, I will stop your mouth." He caught her on the far side of the pool where they could see over the hill to the beaches below. Her top sank to the bottom of the pool. They swam in the darkness, exploring each other until the moon was high in the sky.

Eventually they moved from the water to the wide chaise longue on the lanai. Ty pulled a towel over them, taking the opportunity to kiss her once more. "I love you."

"I love you." She curled up beside him, laying her head on his shoulder. "I have ever since the night in the alley."

"When you rescued me?"

Angela shook her head. "No, before that. When I was riding the motorcycle with you, and then you came walking through the fog to quote Shakespeare for me. When you walked away and I still was waiting for a kiss I realized how fast I'd fallen."

"That was a mistake," he said, pulling her closer.

"Me falling for you?"

"No, that was genius. You should do it every day. Not kissing you was a mistake. To be fair though, I didn't realize what I was missing. Now I know better, and not a day is going to go by that I won't kiss you and tell you how much I love you."

Actor Tyler Running Fox is off the market! Running Fox wed AJ David during an intimate ceremony at her family's estate in Texas. The two have been cast opposite each other in the upcoming production of Much Ado About Nothing *produced by Twelfth Night Films and directed by Susanna Hall.*

THANK YOU!

Dear Reader,

Thank you for taking the time to read this book. I hope you enjoyed reading it as much as I enjoyed writing it.

The best way to support books you love is to spread the word: word of mouth still sells more books than any other method. If you'd like to see more *Heroes and Villains* books, please consider leaving a review at the outlet where you bought this book.

And of course, don't forget to say hi either on Twitter (@lianabrooks), on Facebook (Liana Brooks), or on my blog (www.lianabrooks.com).

Liana

ABOUT THE AUTHOR

Liana Brooks was born in San Diego, California. Years later she was disappointed to learn that The Shire was not some place she could move to, nor was Rider of Rohan an acceptable career choice. Studying marine biology so she could play with sharks seemed to be the only alternative. After college Liana settled down to work as a full-time author and mother because logical career progression is something that happens to other people. When she grows up, Liana wants to be an Evil Overlord and take over the world.

In the meantime, she writes sci fi and SFR in between trips to the beach. She can be found wearing colorful socks on the Emerald Coast, or online at www.lianabrooks.com.

ALSO BY LIANA BROOKS:

EVEN VILLAINS HAVE INTERNS
Heroes & Villains Book #3

It's Chicago's favorite city son vs Delilah, daughter of Dr. Charm. America's second city will never know what hit it.

Available from all major ebook retailers.

Now available in paperback!

www.lianabrooks.com

SNEAK PEEK: EVEN VILLAINS HAVE INTERNS (HEROES & VILLAINS #3)

December 2033

Dear Dad,

Just because Mom mentioned she liked Claude Monet's Grand Canal painting does not mean she wants a copy of it for the house. I know it doesn't mean she wants the original. And telling me not to steal the piece while it's on tour at the Art Institute here in Chicago is not going to convince me to pick it up in time for Christmas. Reverse psychology stopped working when I was twelve.

In other news, you will be happy to learn that Peter Manigault, as painted by Allen Ramsay, mysteriously appeared at the Art Institute this weekend. The curator was very surprised. Personally, I think his shock was more over the two-dollar price tag left on the picture frame than the return of the old painting. It's possible I'm biased.

Locke

DELILAH WATCHED IVAN PETROVICH step toward her on the pier made ghostly by the nighttime gloom. "Don't take it personally, Miss Samson," he said, broken nose still purple from where she'd punched him a week before. "It's not that we don't like you."

"A lot," his companion added. She'd never learned his name. His file was marked 'Snail' because he was always trailing the rest of the gang. "I'd get your autograph if you weren't handcuffed."

A freezing wind whipped the dusting of snow at her feet as Delilah smiled. "Take 'em off, big boy. I bet we can find a pen."

Snail stared, confusion clouding his round face.

Ivan shook his head in frustration. "No. You stay handcuffed, we stay alive. We've been over this."

"This is overkill," Delilah said as icy spray from Lake Michigan bit her ankle. If they pushed her in the water it would be merely waste disposal. With the arctic front that had moved in, all they needed to do to kill her was to leave her outside for another hour.

"You're asking the wrong kinds of questions. Hanging with the wrong kind of people," Ivan said. "I bet your parents warned you about talking to strangers."

"Not as such, no." The shackles around her feet were making life difficult. Ivan had welded them shut before she woke from whatever drug they'd used to give her such a stupendous headache. If she wasn't careful, she was going to lose both her feet tonight. Or her life. She glanced over her shoulder at the water and tried to figure out if the heat from the broken shackles would be tempered enough by the chill of the water to escape with only third degree burns. Physics had never been her favorite subject. "I really think this is a bad plan, boys. If we go through with this, what will we have to do next time we meet? You're escalating the problem. All I want to know is what hit the street. I hate being left out."

Ivan grabbed the lapel of her woolen dress coat, pushing her back so she balanced on her Miu Miu heels. "You should have stayed out of it."

"Don't make me kill you, Ivan. You know what the dry cleaners charge. We go to the same place. Mr. Way is not going to be happy about this."

"But the boss will be. Goodnight, sweetheart." He moved to kiss her and Delilah kicked back, pulling him down into the water with her.

Cold wasn't the right word. Cold was snow-flakes, or iced tea, or the look in her mother's eyes when anyone mentioned Colorado. Lake Michigan in mid-December was a crypt. Death circled, numbing her to the bone. Water poured down her throat as she reflexively gasped for air. Be a mutant freak. Try to save the world. Die of drowning.

Heat burst around her as the shackles fell away. Maybe three seconds had passed. The freezing water had numbed her soul right out of her body. She could almost see herself in the dark water, feebly trying to claw to the surface but sinking anyway because her muscles couldn't move.

Mom is never going to forgive me for this.

The murky darkness of the water became an air-filled darkness bursting with pain. Cold limbs brought to warmth and burning from the change of temperature. Freezing water filled her mouth, her lungs... Air.

There was air! There was the sensation of someone holding her close, and then her knees slammed onto something too hard to be the muddy lake bottom.

Delilah choked, coughed, and vomited out polluted water onto a moonlight-smeared wood floor that bobbed up and down.

None of those words made sense. She made a living out of being sensible, politically aware, and biting her tongue. And yet the floor was bobbing at her. "Th-that's n' ri'." Her teeth chattered. So unbearably cold. Pain. Cold. Heat. Darkness. Movement. She looked up at a shadow, searching for the man it belonged to—but there was no man. No light. Only a shadow. She forced her arms to hug herself for the relief it offered. "'Elp?"

"I can get you a blanket," the shadow said.

"'Es." Hot tears burned her face. She was alive.

Anger burst through the pain. Ivan was going to regret this night for the rest of his foreshortened life. She'd make sure of that.

Ivan. Snail. The mayor. In her mind she lined up the rogue's gallery. Dealing drugs out of rehab centers, now that took a twisty kind of mind. The city

tried to reduce street crime by sending minor off-
enders to weekend rehabilitation instead of jail, and
what did those hoodlums go home with? A nice
duffle bag full of pamphlets, clean underwear, and
dime bags of meth.

But something more was happening. The thriv-
ing Chicago sub-economy had gone quiet in the past
few weeks, like birds before a storm. Or the jungle
when an apex predator stalked past. She thought
she'd finally caught a break when Ivan and Snail
scheduled a meet down on West Wacker. All the
evidence was on the camera...

The camera!

She struggled to stand and started stripping off
her wet clothes. If the camera was ruined... *Argh! Ivan
you idiot, why couldn't you off me in the normal way?* His
modus operandi was leaving people 'drunk' and
stripped in one of the parks. The cops logged it as a
partygoer who'd wandered off and been killed by
Chicago's infamous weather. It happened. It was a
shame. No crime though. Why'd he have to change
his style now?

Because you're a freak, she reminded herself.   The
usual drugs didn't affect her strange body chemistry.

"Um..." The man's voice was behind her. "I found
a towel if you want... Should I leave?" he asked as
she threw her shirt to the side and slid out of her
pants.

Pocket. Fingers. Cold fingers never worked the
way she wanted. Why couldn't the goons have been

operating in Miami? This was it. This was definitely going to be her last winter in Chicago. In March she'd ask for the raise and a transfer to the Subrosa Securities offices somewhere warm. The French Riviera maybe. Or Spain. Or... somewhere.

She wiggled out of her boots and dug her fingers into the lining where she'd slid the ultra-thin camera as soon as she'd realized someone was following her. *Hot dog!* With shaking hands she patted it dry. There. Good. Evidence. Now...

Her teeth started chattering again.

A warm, scratchy blanket was laid over her shoulders. Delilah looked down, saw a cord... followed the cord to a little green light.

"Heating blanket," the shadow said. He faded into the corner. "I know you're not a native, but we figure even tourists should know better than to swim in Lake Michigan in the middle of winter. That's why it's not posted on the docks next to the prominent 'Keep Out—Authorized Personnel Only' signs."

Delilah's fist clenched around the camera. "Th-thanks. Silly me." She sucked in cool air. "Where are we?"

"A boat."

Good. Locations were good. "Yours?"

"No."

"Mine?"

"Not that I'm aware of."

All right then. She nodded. "Phone?"

"I don't keep one on me. Makes me feel like I'm wearing a leash. It's good to get away from the day job, don't you think?"

She gave him her best *shut up* glare, perfected on her four siblings over the past two decades, and staggered toward a wall. Walls meant doors. Doors meant halls. Halls meant communications devices of some kind. Boats had phones, or computers, or radios, something like that. Her sum knowledge of boats was they were supposed to float, holes were bad, and boats talked to other boats. Ergo, help and warm clothes were just down the hall. And possibly up a flight of stairs.

"Where are you going?" the shadow asked.

"Help. Got to get help." She huffed on her cupped hands to warm them. There was a pop behind her as the heating blanket came unplugged. How inconvenient.

The shadow bent down and plugged it back in. "Sit down. I'll go find a phone. And some clothes."

A real gentleman would have offered his coat. Not that her mysterious rescuer seemed to have one. If he was who she was beginning to suspect he was, he didn't need one. Ghosts didn't need anything to keep the chill off.

Delilah sat on a vinyl bench and looked at the city skyline through a narrow rectangular window. Willis Tower was lit up for the holidays, bright, festive, and a beacon of hope north of her. So, 31st Street Harbor.

Good. The cab could be here in a matter of minutes. She leaned back.

"Got a problem here," said the shadow as he entered the room. "The clothes are a bit big and these shoes…" He held up a pair of bright pink satin pumps in a lady's size twenty. Both her feet could have fit in one with room left over.

"Everyone needs a hobby." The words came out clearly between her chattering teeth. "Phone?"

"Nothing. I guess whoever comes here likes their privacy."

"Fine. I'll walk. Give me the clothes."

He held out a matching pink-sequined dress that was too big, bright, and cheap to ever be in her wardrobe.

"And here I thought I'd have to join the circus to wear something this tacky." At least the sleeves were long. Too long. Like an over-sized sweater made in the middle of a sequin explosion. "Thanks for the lift. It was nice not seeing you. Enjoy your evening." She pulled the heating blanket's plug deliberately this time, folded the blanket neatly, and made a mental note to send one of the interns down to the docks with a small remuneration and the dress for the owner.

"Mind telling me what you were up to tonight?" The shadow followed her down the creaky hall.

"Chasing bad guys, busting drug deals, getting evidence. You know, do-gooder stuff."

"You think you're a superhero?"

Ha. "Nope. You are though, right? The Spirit of Chicago, our city's favorite son. I saw the news segment you did in the graveyard last year. No record of birth, no name, no physical body, although you've just demonstrated your ability to lift things up, so I have to wonder how much of that was staged."

The shadows where his face should have been changed, shading to mimic the expression of a surprised man. "Says the woman who impersonates Harry Houdini as a Christmas Party trick." He sighed. "What's your name?"

"At home?"

The Rosencrantz and Guildenstern reference flew right over his head. "On your Company file."

"Locke." She smiled sweetly over her shoulder. "But I'm not listed as a superhero."

"The villain?" He swore so softly she would have missed it if she weren't expecting it.

"That's me."

"What are you doing chasing drug dealers? Did they cut you out of something?"

Delilah rolled her eyes. "No, I was chasing them because you suck at your job. Your ability to catch actual criminals is matched only by your ability to stop time and speed up the harvest. You've never done anything but haunt people." She leaned against the rail. "Do you know what time it is?"

"Hot date?"

"No." Her date was lukewarm at best, and being stood up for the third time. Hopefully the mayor's righthand man would get the point. Every time she ran into him, she fought the urge to stab his eyes out of spite. Alan Adale was the snake of Eden walking around in the body of a fallen angel. He had asked her if she was free for dinner tonight in front of people. There'd been no way to wiggle out of it without losing her standing.

Besides, the local tabloids already had them pegged as Chicago's next Power Couple, as if that was something to be proud of. She was pretty sure Adale was up to his handsome neck in whatever was going down. "Time?"

"Quarter to eleven. You missed Doctor Who, but you should be able to catch a rerun of the Firefly reboot."

"Unlikely. I need to catch a plane. My intern is flying in," she elaborated when he tilted his head.

"Super villains have interns?"

"Well, superheroes have the whole sidekick thing pretty well wrapped up. I guess you could call him a minion, but since he's being paid instead of exploited, I went with intern." And if she missed his flight and left her sister's favorite student of all time stranded at O'Hare airport... Angela had doted on the boy even before he'd shot her in the arm. When he'd come to Angela's wedding over the summer, he'd mentioned he was having weird premonitions. Like called to like. Delilah'd asked some questions and, sure enough, Big Sis's favorite kid was a genetic freak too. His powers were minor, premonitions of when people were going to die and the ability to heal a little faster than normal humans. It wasn't enough to win him a spot in The Company as a superhero, but it would be enough to earn him a visit from their silencing squad if they ever found out about him.

Delilah and Angela's family had closed ranks around the boy, herding him in like they had Angela's husband and brother-in-law. Travys was safe. And once he'd enrolled in the University of Chicago, she'd pulled a few strings to get him a place as her intern for a few months. It was the only way to train him to survive.

The shadow sauntered closer. "Where do you need to go? I can drop you off at home."

"I don't take boys home on the first date, or ghosts home ever. My ride will be here shortly."

An icy breeze fluttered her hair. Behind the shadow a man in a tight blue suit landed, face covered by a sculpted mask that horribly disfigured the handsome man beneath. Not the ride she'd expected. "My ears are burning. Were you talking about me?" he asked with a smile.

She could picture Ty raising an eyebrow behind his mask.

"Cute dress," her brother-in-law said. "Angela will be jealous."

"Long story. How'd you know I needed a lift?"

"Frederick called to tell us you were out of communication. I came out and waited. Who's the new boyfriend?"

"The Spirit of Chicago, and not my boyfriend." She walked over to her brother-in-law, waving careless fingers over her shoulder. "Toodles."

The shadow gave her a lazy salute. "Some other time, perhaps."

"Perhaps."

Ty moved fast, dropping her at the apartment and flying her to the airport once she'd changed. He hovered in the shadows. "You sure you're fine?"

"I'm perfect. No lingering affects except an abiding desire to get home and snuggle under my quilt with the heater turned up to eighty. Freddie is bringing the cab around. I'll drop Travys at his dorm room and go straight home. Which is where you should go," she added firmly. "Your home. Drop the camera off with Daddy on your way, please."

He laughed. "You need to go get your own errand boy."

"I have twelve minions and an intern who eats like a horse."

"Why don't you co-opt that shadow dude? He's here, why can't he work for us?"

Delilah smiled wryly. "Us being the good guys who fight the other good guys for a chance to fight the bad guys? There is no 'us', Ty. Maybe you and

Angela have California tied up, but the Midwest isn't going to suddenly see the light and flee the strangling embrace of The Company. I'm not sure the Spirit of Chicago could. He's supposed to be the ghost of someone who died in the Chicago fire."

"He looked solid to me."

"Yeah." To her too. "I'll worry about it later. Kisses to Angela, tell Aaron I say hi."

"No more adventures before Christmas," Ty said. "Angela's been sleeping poorly enough as it is."

"Oh?" Delilah glanced up, although Ty's masked face gave no hints.

He shrugged. "Nightmares about what happened with Jacob. She wakes up screaming about fires. Not frequent, but between that and the stomach bug going around it's been a rough week."

She nodded. "No more adventures. Promise. I will not do anything thrilling, heroic, or risky for the next two weeks. Girl Scout's honor." A plane rumbled overhead, coming in to land. "That should be Travys. Have a good night." She smiled and walked into the lobby before Ty could remember she'd never been a Girl Scout.

The warm, stale air of the terminal was almost comforting. Still, she shivered. Nightmares were the bane of her existence. First her mother's memories of the time she was kidnapped and mind-raped in Colorado, and now her sister's memories of the man she couldn't save. She'd unlocked those, stolen them in unguarded moments, and they'd become part of her even though they weren't her experiences. A midnight swim in Lake Michigan just couldn't compete. So she tucked the fear out of the way, and moved forward. A super villain's work was never done.

Head to
www.inkprintpress.com/
lianabrooks/heroesandvillains/interns/
to keep reading today!

www.ingramcontent.com/pod-product-compliance
Lightning Source LLC
Chambersburg PA
CBHW070937190726

48292CB00004B/1215